FOR LOVE AND CHARITY

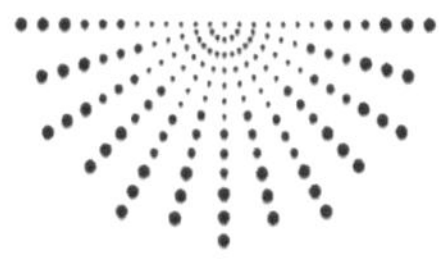

ALISON JOY

DRAGONFLY BLUE ENTERPRISES

Managing editor: Belinda Pollard

Proofreader: Alix Kwan

Cover design by Belinda Pollard

Cover images copyright © Wavebreak Media Ltd via Bigstock and © Tom Merton/KOTO via Adobe Stock

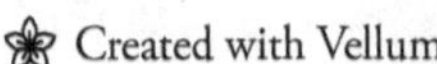 Created with Vellum

For **C.A.R.D.S**

CHAPTER ONE

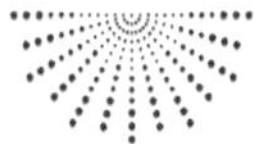

1997—SOMEWHERE OVER THE CENTRAL PACIFIC OCEAN

The aircraft had become smaller and smaller with each successive flight, the closer Laura Maxwell got to the remote Pacific island of Levati. Heading north from Australia via Singapore, she had simply hung a right at Guam and kept going.

The electric blues of the ocean fascinated her as the sun sparkled over the expanse of water. Even with sunglasses, the brightness hurt her eyes.

As the only white female among the handful of passengers in the twin-prop Beechcraft King cargo plane, she was heading to Levati's southernmost medical facility, on one of the main outer islands. The passenger in front of her pointed out a smudge on the horizon. "Levati," was his single-word explanation. The smudge became more defined and grew into a landform. The plane banked above pristine white beaches, majestic palm trees, and native dwellings built over the water.

But Laura knew the peaceful appearance was deceptive. Since gaining independence, the tiny nation seemed to have gone from bad to worse. A corrupt government had destroyed the fledgling tourist industry with excessive demands to satisfy its greed. A rebel force under a former army commander had tried to bring down the government, resulting in civil war. Hapless islanders were caught between the two feuding groups.

At the moment, an uneasy truce prevailed, though minor skirmishes broke out from time to time. A US military outpost on the far side of this island kept out of the local fighting as much as possible, but helped with road building, and establishing water supplies and electricity.

Despite the extensive induction sessions before Laura embarked on the journey from her hometown in Brisbane, she was facing the unknown. As the plane lined up its approach to the tiny airstrip, she braced herself, not only for the landing but for the twelve weeks ahead.

FEELING like a wilted flower in the oppressive humidity, Laura stretched her cramped and tired muscles. Retying her long dark hair, she secured it up off the back of her neck, and glanced around the ramshackle building that served as the airport terminal. The erratic thump of cargo hitting the tarmac at the back of the plane caught her attention. She followed the other passengers to the rear, hauled her suitcase out of the growing pile and set it upright, slotting her cabin bag onto the handle.

Heat radiated from the ground and snaked around her body. Sweat started its slide down her back. She flapped the front of her shirt away from her skin in a futile attempt to get some air circulating.

As she approached an old dark-green Land Rover, lugging her bags, a short, dark, wiry man ambled over.

"Er, Miss Maxwell?"

"Yes, that's right."

"Toby Oliver from the hospital." His English was accented but understandable.

She set her bag down and took his outstretched hand. "Pleased to meet you."

A line of men arrived, each carrying a box to be stowed in the open back of the Land Rover. Some contained fruit and vegetables. The rest, she guessed, might be other foodstuffs or medical supplies. The stack grew alarmingly high, like one of those crazy board games that involved stacking chairs.

Toby swung her suitcase onto the top without even tying it down. Laura clambered in as he started the engine, and grabbed at the top edge of the door as he lurched off then tore along what amounted to no more than a bush track. She prayed her bags wouldn't fly off the back as they hurtled through the jungle growth.

Ten hair-raising minutes later, the vehicle roared through the open chainwire gates of the secure hospital compound. The Land Rover screeched to a halt in front of a white demountable building fifty metres behind the main hospital. Toby leapt out and, by the time Laura caught up, was already carrying her bags up half a dozen stairs, through a screen door and into the staff quarters. On the right, a flyscreen-enclosed area held half a dozen cane chairs. He opened one of a row of doors on the left, and set her bags down.

"Thanks, Mr Oliver." She smiled at him.

"Humpf." He walked back out and drove off in a cloud of dust.

A grateful sigh escaped her lips as she stepped into the relative cool of her white-painted room. It was small but clean with dark blue vinyl flooring. There was a metal single bed along one side, and a cupboard and small timber desk built into the opposite wall. A dark blue plastic chair sat under the bench. She sat on the bed with its single pillow and turquoise bedspread. Comfortable enough for her three months on the island as volunteer nurse for Medi-Aid. At a loss to know what else to do, she started to unpack.

There was a knock on her door. A forty-something woman with short, wavy brown hair and glasses was stuffing a stethoscope into the pocket of her white coat. She wore long navy dress shorts topped with a brightly patterned tropical print blouse, similar to the one Laura had spied in her wardrobe.

"Laura?"

"Yes, that's right." She stood to greet the woman.

"I'm Doctor Angela Reid from Adelaide, and I'm in charge here. Well at least I will be for the next thirteen days, seven hours and"—she looked at her watch—"twenty-four minutes."

"Oh?"

"I miss my family," she conceded. "This is my fourth stint. As much as I enjoy the work, it's a long time to be away from the kids. Come on, I'll show you around." They fell into step as they crossed the compound. "So, you only get to put up with me for a little while before Marcus Bradley takes over. This whole thing is his baby, really. He and his father head a consortium of medical people who raised the money to rebuild the hospital. His father is a well-known neurosurgeon."

"David Bradley?"

"That's the one. He's a close friend of Charles Ogilvie."

"I heard Doctor Ogilvie speak in Brisbane." At an age when most men would be contemplating retirement, the eminent surgeon and founder of the relief organisation Medi-Aid International had been recruiting volunteer medical personnel for war-torn countries. Before she quite realised what she had done, Laura had signed up, been interviewed and accepted, and had arranged leave, convinced she needed to step out of her comfort zone.

"Doctor Ogilvie can tell some pretty compelling stories," Angela said. "David and Marcus head up Medi-Aid International in this region. David's other son Stephen is a lawyer, and he handles all that side of things."

"It must be a huge commitment."

"David is pretty much retired now. Still does consulting work. Marcus has a thriving practice in North Queensland. He's a particularly gifted surgeon, so he's in big demand, but he still finds time to do his three-month stint here every year."

Angela pulled open the back door to the lowset hospital building, where a generator drowned out other sounds. They passed the staff common room, pharmacy, offices and doctor accommodation on their way down the narrow hall to the main entrance.

"Well, here we are. I can give you a quick tour"—Angela checked her watch again—"before the next clinic starts, and then you can go get yourself settled."

The hospital, built to take advantage of the local climatic conditions, was surprisingly cool inside. It looked like any small country hospital back home. The vinyl flooring was the same dark blue as her room—no doubt a nod to the tropical waters around the island. The nurses' station was dark grey. The work of local artists featured around the pale blue walls. Simple brush-strokes combined to create intricate works in keeping with the simple, clean lines of the hospital. Chairs lined the walls either side, between the doors to the consultation rooms. The three wards beyond held a total of twenty-four beds.

"We have a well-equipped theatre." The older woman opened its doors. Laura couldn't help but be impressed. They seemed to be in a position to deal with most emergencies. "Having a talented surgeon at the forefront of fundraising has given us a set up other Medi-Aid centres can only dream of."

"Sounds like he must almost qualify for sainthood around here."

Angela laughed. "Marcus Bradley, a saint? Hardly. But I'll say this, his determination to ease the plight of the people on Levati is second to none. Don't get in his way or you risk getting steamrolled."

Laura considered herself warned.

Doctor Reid handed her a thick folder of policies and procedures. "Here's some light reading for you."

Laura took the folder and found her way back out. She discovered the kitchen in a separate building joined to the hospital by a short, covered walkway. A cold room was attached to the back of the kitchen. Just to the right of the building was some rough bench seating in the shade of a cluster of trees. A sand-filled metal container nearby held the remnants of cigarettes. She followed the path back up the gentle slope past a concrete-block laundry where washing machines clanked away. The clothes lines supported by T-shaped wooden posts were like those she'd seen in vintage photos.

A grey concrete amenities block stood between several identical buildings that housed sleeping quarters. Two Land Rovers were parked under trees, alongside a truck that had seen better days. In a nearby workshop, half a dozen men were busy repairing machinery of some sort.

Security floodlights hanging from high poles would light her way to the hospital at night. Laura headed back to her room. From the small window over her bed, she saw the security fence that enclosed the compound, and beyond it, thick jungle.

Laura hit it off with Angela Reid. Too bad the good doctor would be heading home soon.

An emergency appendectomy was the first operation she assisted Angela with, on just her second day. There were other scheduled trips to theatre. The two of them quickly fell into a comfortable pattern. Laura relished the challenge of theatre work and was able to make suggestions to Doctor Reid to help streamline some of her processes. Angela wasn't as comfortable in the operating theatre, and she commented more than once how much she appreciated Laura's calm efficiency. They had the makings of a good team.

Laura enjoyed getting to know local people as they lined up for the daily clinic. The children won her over with their shy smiles, despite their pain and discomfort.

Immunisations played a big part in the treatment of children and adults alike. Locals tended to view the interlopers warily, and it had been an uphill battle to convince them to use the facilities. Training locals had gone a long way to improving relations, and part of Laura's job was training nurses' aides. Some were eager to learn, but for others she had to work harder to motivate them. Several spoke a little English, and with a lot of gestures and miming Laura seemed to communicate well.

Over the first few days, Laura met the rest of the team, who went out of their way to help her fit in. In total, there were about twenty staff. Some had signed up for three months, others for longer. The logistician, administrator and head engineer were paid positions, but the rest were all volunteers.

One wall of the common room was given over to photos of those who had worked on the island over the years. Laura studied names and countries of origin. Although most seemed to be from Australia and New Zealand, it was a mini United Nations. Doctor Bradley's photo was conspicuous by its absence.

Laura thumbed through the dog-eared stack of books on offer, looking for something to read in her down time.

"Hey Laura. Are you staying for the movie tonight?"

"Um, yeah, sure," she replied.

As usual, the common room was crowded with people. It didn't matter that the comedy wasn't the latest release. It helped lift everyone's spirits to have a good laugh. Laura chuckled along with everyone else.

They all worked hard to maintain a good working atmosphere. No doubt there would be issues and personality clashes, but for now Laura made an effort to get along with everyone.

∼

BARELY A WEEK after she'd arrived, Laura was chatting to the other nurse on duty at the reception desk when there was a flurry of excitement from her colleagues.

"The cargo plane just flew over," she was told.

Laura picked up the top piece of paper from the pile in front of her and went on with her work, not understanding why the plane's arrival was such a big deal.

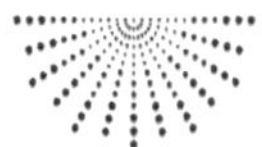

CHAPTER TWO

Marcus Bradley watched the familiar form of the airfield at Levati take shape as they came in to land. He rubbed a hand over the stubble on his face and wiped his tired eyes. The trip never got any easier, despite the number of times he'd been here since they had finally got the hospital up and running. His heavy operating schedule before he flew out hadn't helped.

At least he could count on a shower and a decent night's sleep before he had to be on deck. Hopefully, he'd have a few days to ease himself back into the change of pace that was his life when he was here.

Angela would be champing at the bit to get out on next week's plane, though. Not that he could blame her. Leaving a husband and kids behind for that length of time was always the downside, as it was for many of the staff leaving loved ones behind. For his own part, he missed his nephew and nieces the most—Stephen and Danielle's kids. And his widowed father. At this stage of his life he was grateful not to have a wife and his own children. His work hours were crazy, and he was thankful the other partners in his practice recognised the value of what he was doing here on the ground in Levati, tolerating his annual leave of absence.

The brilliant blue of the water drew his attention as it always did. To walk along the sand at the end of a long shift always rejuvenated him. Sand and water—the main reasons he pushed so hard for the rebuild of the hospital here in Levati.

The plane swayed as the pilot lined the craft up with the runway. It bounced a couple of times as it hit the ground, pulled up in quick time, and swung around to the small white building that passed as the terminal.

Angela Reid had heard the telltale drone of the cargo plane from her office desk, knowing that the arrival of Doctor Bradley would cause a bit of excitement among the female staff, as it always did. No doubt there would be last-minute preening going on, and the old hands would be enlightening the newbies.

She had spent a good deal of time working with Marcus on Levati. The previous year they had two months on the island at the same time. He was affable and totally dedicated to his work, especially the hospital here on Levati. The fact that he was easy on the eye didn't hurt, although he seemed totally unaware of the interest he generated in the female staff, young or old, married or not.

A while later she noticed the unmistakable sound of Toby Oliver and his Land Rover roaring into the compound, and braced herself for the charm offensive. Angela heard someone she assumed was Marcus walk by the half-closed storeroom door a few minutes later. She continued to work down the list of items on the clipboard in front of her, pulling them off the shelf and setting them aside, intending to let the initial fuss of his arrival die down before she made an appearance.

LAURA WAS ENGROSSED in the pile of paperwork on her desk when she became aware of a growing commotion at the front of the hospital. A noise on the other side of the counter caught her attention. She looked up to see a pair of vivid blue eyes regarding her from under a shock of blond wavy hair. Unshaven, and casually dressed in an unbuttoned blue polo shirt that intensified the colour of his eyes, the man looked totally out of place. Like a tourist who'd gotten lost between the beach and the resort. But there was no resort around here.

Her glance took in the cheap black plastic watch on his wrist, at odds with the gold signet ring on the little finger of his right hand. He hooked a pair of sunglasses into the opening of his shirt.

"Hello, I'm Doctor—" He stopped mid-sentence, his attention arrested by a disturbance at the main entrance. Laura followed his gaze. "Looks like we've got trouble," he finished.

Well, she did, that's for sure. Her "at rest" pulse rate had headed for the hills. A flutter of Wandering Butterflies, like those she'd noticed in the hospital grounds, started to do just that in her midsection—wander. Her stomach muscles tightened in a vain effort to keep them from taking flight. How could he possibly have had an instant effect on her?

Dropping the large black duffle bag from his shoulder, he darted off. She barely had time to register it must be *the* Doctor Bradley before he was back, alongside a makeshift stretcher carried by two young men in worn, faded t-shirts and baggy, ripped shorts. The male patient was covered in blood and the doctor's hands were already stained.

"We've got a stabbing," he shouted. "C'mon, Nurse." Laura left her post and joined the doctor as he made his way down the corridor, listening for his instructions.

As Marcus pushed through the doors into the theatre, Angela Reid came in behind the dark-haired nurse. The one with the melt-your-insides chocolate brown eyes that he'd locked onto for the briefest of seconds. He had already registered that she was very attractive, and that he wouldn't mind getting to know her better, but he pushed the thoughts aside as he shepherded the stretcher bearers out of the room.

Laura ran to help the doctors scrub up. She found it difficult to get into stride and struggled to meet the needs of those she was attending. Doctor Bradley worked with practised ease. Laura had no idea why now, of all times, when the main driving force of the hospital was in attendance, she was struggling so much. It was so unlike her and not a good first impression, that's for sure.

"Nurse!" he commanded impatiently, time after time.

"Sorry, Doctor," she apologised, and handed him the required instrument. She felt as awkward and clumsy as when she had started her training all those years ago. Trying to focus in, she knew she would be relieved to see the final suture in place.

It wasn't hard for Angela to notice Laura wasn't her usual self today, but then neither was Doctor Bradley. Tired, obviously, after the long flights—but there was something else that she couldn't quite put her finger on. Poor Sister Maxwell was copping the full brunt of whatever was going on. She wanted badly to intervene, but her first priority was the patient. The other stuff would have to wait until later.

The doctor looked across at Laura as he finished. "How long have you been here, Nurse..."

"Maxwell," Angela Reid put in smoothly. "Laura Maxwell."

"Just a week," Laura told him.

Shaking his head as he peeled off his surgical gloves and gown, he seemed about to launch into a tirade of some sort.

"Back off, Marcus," Angela warned him. "You're not at Calvary now."

Muttering something under his breath, he pushed the patient through to the recovery room. Angela came up to where Laura was standing. "Don't feel so bad. He's used to working with a team who know his every movement almost before he does. It takes some adjustment on both sides. You were fine."

Laura slowly started cleaning up the mess, not sure if she appreciated Angela standing up to Doctor Bradley on her behalf. Her hands were shaking as she went about her job. The whole debacle replayed in her head over and over. What must he think of her? There was no logical explanation for her performance just now. She was bitterly disappointed that her first encounter with Doctor Bradley would be memorable for all the wrong reasons.

MARCUS LEANED on the edge of the brown laminated desk in Angela's—soon to be his again—office. Cramped but mostly in order, except for the inevitable pile on the far end of the table-top. He ran a distracted hand through his hair and tried to collect his scattered thoughts. The nurse had about done his head in—in five seconds flat. It must be because he was tired. Yeah that was it. Had to be. The only logical explanation.

He was disappointed the pretty face hadn't been able to keep up in surgery. What were they thinking, letting someone like her onto the island? In this hospital? His hospital? Surely, they weren't so hard up for volunteers that they would take just anyone. Or maybe she had just flashed those brown eyes at the interviewers, and they had acquiesced without even bothering to check her references. That had to be it.

He blew a breath out. It was going to be a long three

months. He crossed his arms defensively as his colleague walked into the room.

~

ANGELA DIDN'T BEAT around the bush. "What on earth just happened in there?" she asked.

He shrugged, rubbing at the back of his neck as he pushed himself off the desk and started pacing the small room.

"I think you were a bit hard on her, Marc. You came in here without so much as a hello and started barking out orders and whatnot. You probably unsettled her."

"If she's experienced enough, she should be able to cope, regardless of what's thrown at her. How did she even get here? We have a pretty tough list of qualifications needed before someone can volunteer here. Does she even have the necessary experience? Did she slip through the net somehow?"

Wow, he's worked up. "Maybe you should have cut her some slack. You weren't exactly firing on all cylinders in there yourself." He looked up sharply. She put her hand up to pacify him. "Knowing you, you were probably operating up until you got on the plane. Heck, they probably had to hold the flight for you." Ha, she was spot on and she knew it.

"Sorry, Angela, was I that bad?" He stopped pacing and looked at her questioningly.

Seriously, he had no idea? "It's not me you need to apologise to."

He sighed and stretched his head back, rubbing at his neck again. She regarded him for a minute and then it dawned on her. Someone had gotten under his skin. Granted he was tired, but the normally unflappable, laid-back doctor was rattled. Angela was delighted by this turn of events. This could be interesting.

But for now, she had to smooth some ruffled feathers. She crossed to the desk, flicking her finger down the files before pulling one of many cream-coloured folders from the pile.

"Laura Maxwell is actually very highly regarded. Here, you can read it for yourself." She tossed the folder on to the other end of the desk toward him and headed for the door. She paused on the way out, intending to say something else, but thought better of it.

MARCUS FLICKED open the file and sat down to check out Nurse Maxwell. A few minutes and he was done. Angela was right, Laura Maxwell was highly regarded. In fact, her resume was damn impressive. It seemed improbable that she could have imploded just like that. He threw the folder back onto the pile. He would seek her out later and make amends. But first, he needed to unpack, gather his thoughts, and have a shower. Man, he needed one badly.

CHAPTER THREE

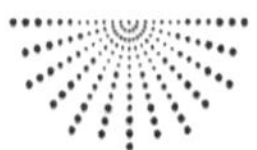

By the time Laura finished her shift, Doctor Bradley was regaling the gathered staff members with some amusing anecdote. She skirted the group crowded around the joined tables and quietly made herself a sandwich. There was a white demarcation line around the edge of the bread slices where staleness was migrating inwards from the crust—even though it would have arrived with the supplies today. Slathering it with a spread would make it more palatable.

The hospital staff were fortunate that a weekly delivery of fresh food helped make the stay more bearable, but she hated to think of the cost of bringing in supplies.

Taking a piece of fruit from the bowl, she slipped outside. The cool of the evening air soothed her tiredness as she made her way back up to the screened veranda of the sleeping quarters and gratefully sank into a chair without turning on a light. A few minutes later, she put the empty plate down and closed her eyes, listening to the multitude of night sounds all around. Some were becoming familiar. So different from the ones of suburban Brisbane. She still didn't know what they all were, and made a mental note to ask someone.

Making a conscious effort to slow her breathing, she relaxed into the back of the low-slung chair.

Her peace was disturbed when the screen door snapped back. She didn't want to acknowledge the intruder, but knew she should. Opening her eyes, she saw a pair of casual shoes and bare legs. She stomped on her body's involuntary response before it had a chance to get out of hand. Her eyes travelled upwards, noting, even in the dark, the potent outline of Marcus Bradley as he stood towering over her. They regarded each other warily.

He spoke first. "We didn't get off to a very good start this afternoon. Do you mind if we start again?" His deep voice spoke quietly, a complete contrast to the one that had barked orders at her in the operating theatre. It sent a surge of… something… coursing through her.

Her nod was almost imperceptible.

"Doctor Marcus Bradley." He held out a hand to her which she took reluctantly. She almost jumped at the shock of static electricity that hit her as his hand enfolded hers.

"Laura Maxwell." *Let my hand go.*

The doctor finally withdrew his hand, but oddly she wanted to grasp it right back.

"So how long have you been on Levati?"

"I got here last week."

"And how are you enjoying it so far?"

"Fine," she replied. "Up until this afternoon," she added before she could stop herself. He ignored her comment.

"How long have you been nursing?"

Laura took this as an attack on her ability. "Twelve years," she told him, getting to her feet. "Look, Doctor Bradley, I'm sorry I wasn't up to scratch in the theatre this afternoon." She could feel her heart rate escalating. "Everyone is entitled to a bad day now and then. If you'll excuse me, I need to get some sleep. I'm on early tomorrow." As she moved away, she couldn't help herself. "I'm sure Doctor Reid will let you check out my references, if you haven't already done so."

Sidestepping him quickly, she escaped to her room, leaning

back on the closed door until she heard the telltale bang of the screen door shutting. She took several deep breaths, and her heart rate slowly returned to its normal pace.

ANGELA REID POSITIONED herself in the staffroom so she would be able to see both Laura and the senior doctor when he arrived to start the meeting. Laura sat at the back, apparently trying to be as inconspicuous as possible.

Marcus Bradley strode in, clipboard in hand at the front of the room, checking through his notes as the chatter quietened. He started talking before he looked up, but when he did, he seemed distracted. Just momentarily, but Angela noticed.

He scowled and continued, repositioning himself ever so slightly, so Laura was out of his direct line of vision. Angela smiled to herself. Her young friend was looking everywhere but at the speaker in front, and moving uncomfortably in her seat. Laura leaned her chin on one elbow, flipped a notebook open and began doodling around the edges.

LISTEN *but don't look up*, Laura kept telling herself. But she couldn't help stealing glances every so often. Then he made eye contact, just for the briefest of seconds, really. Embarrassingly, she felt colour rising to her cheeks, and she had to fight to drop her gaze away from the intensity of those eyes. Even from a distance they impacted her equilibrium.

MARCUS BRADLEY WAS FIGHTING himself not to look at the dark-haired nurse who had affected him so much in such a short space of time. He wasn't sure why exactly. When he'd shaken her hand last night, he had felt an instant connection to her. Weird. Nothing like that had ever happened to him before. Now he was struggling to get through a simple staff meeting which he should have been able to do blindfolded. On second thoughts, maybe blindfolded was a good idea, then he couldn't get distracted by those pretty brown eyes.

~

DOCTOR BRADLEY WAS NOWHERE to be seen around the hospital. Laura was relieved, but not able to relax. After her shift, Angela suggested a walk to the beach.

"You're kidding, right?" Laura said in disbelief. How could that even be a thing?

"No, it's only about a five-minute stroll from here."

"Is it safe?"

The older woman nodded. "Most of the trouble you've probably heard about is four or five hours from here. Often, we just see the end results here at the hospital. We're perfectly safe."

Laura changed into long, faded, dark blue denim cut off shorts and a pink tank top.

After plaiting her hair, she slathered on sunscreen, and grabbed her straw hat and sunglasses before meeting her new friend. Angela was wearing light blue chambray shorts that tied at the waist. Her black tank top was covered by an unbuttoned, red, short-sleeved shirt. The hat she wore was much wider than Laura's.

Laura was glad Doctor Reid had decided to take her under her wing. She wasn't looking forward to Angela's impending departure.

They followed a well-worn path through thick vegetation. Laura could hear voices shouting, growing louder as they walked. Angela didn't seem concerned.

Emerging down a slight hill onto the narrow expanse of gleaming pale sand, they came across an active game of Ultimate

Frisbee. Laura followed Angela as they picked their way over to a shady spot to sit and observe the action.

It was easy to distinguish the two teams. One side wore shirts. The others were without.

Doctor Bradley was shirtless. Despite being very tanned, next to the island youths he was lily white. He'd spun his cap backwards to see the frisbee better and was setting a fast pace for the others. From the broad, muscled shoulders and chest down to the narrow waist and brief black shorts, Laura had to admit to herself he was one good-looking doctor. Her companion apparently agreed.

"What a hot bod," Angela sighed, as Doctor Bradley dived for the disc.

"Angela!"

"Don't look so shocked, Laura. Just because I'm on a diet doesn't mean I can't look at the menu. Oh, if I was only ten years younger…"

"Doctor Reid, I can't believe you meant that."

"Okay, I admit that I'm more than happy with my Don, but he's not one hundred percent beefcake like the good doctor over there."

"I'm sure Doctor Bradley would be thrilled to know you think of him in those terms."

The disc flew from player to player as it made its way up and down the beach. She had seen a few games at uni, and quickly picked up the flow of play. As much as she tried to resist, her gaze was continually drawn to the doctor as he pivoted, ran, threw the disc and occasionally pulled a layout. He was all-in, all the time. His skin gleamed with moisture.

Her mouth was suddenly dry, and she licked her lips. She could feel the heat rising on her face. Whew, it was warm out today.

They watched until the game finished. There were high-fives all around and the group started to disperse. Marcus Bradley tipped his cap and tucked it under one arm while he grabbed a hand towel that had been hanging over a tree branch, wiping the sweat from his face and neck before giving himself a quick rub down. He leaned down and picked up his grey t-shirt, walking towards them as he slipped it on, flicked the towel over his shoulder and settled his cap back on the right way.

"Ladies," he acknowledged when he got closer. "Mind if I walk back with you?" He held out a hand which Angela accepted, and he hauled her to her feet. Laura ignored his proffered arm. Not wanting to run the risk of another adverse reaction from his touch, she scrambled up under her own steam.

The two doctors caught up on hospital news while Laura kept to herself, walking a couple of paces behind. Something was unsettling her, and she had no idea what it was. She was miles away when she realised someone had spoken to her.

"What? Sorry."

"Marcus and I are going into the village. Why don't you come along?'

"Thanks, but I don't think—"

"Nonsense, we won't take no for an answer, will we, Marcus?"

"Well, if Ms Maxwell would rather not…"

Of course I'd rather not. I'd rather be anywhere else. "I, er…" There was no easy out and she couldn't be rude to Angela, especially as she'd gone out of her way to include her. "Okay," she finally managed.

"If you don't mind, I think I'll go and grab a quick shower first." Marcus Bradley jogged ahead.

"Give him a break, Laura. He's not that bad. You might even get to like him." Angela's pager beeped. "Oh bother, I've got to go. I'll be back soon." She hurried along the path ahead of Laura.

Taking her time to reach the staff quarters, Laura wandered over to sit on one of the crudely-fashioned timber benches in the shade. A short time later, Doctor Bradley emerged from the hospital building and strode over to her, damp hair slicked back.

The white, very fitted t-shirt he wore bore the stylised stethoscope of the Medi-Aid logo. Baggy khaki cargo shorts and running shoes without socks made him seem like he was on his way to play a round of golf or maybe some tennis.

"Ready?" he asked.

"What about Doctor Reid?" Laura said.

"Been held up. She'll have to take a raincheck."

"Look, I don't want to put you out…"

"It's no bother. C'mon."

The small of her back tingled when he placed a hand there and guided her over to one of the two Land Rovers parked behind the hospital. The fresh smell of his cologne weaved around her defences as he moved past her to pull on the handle of the passenger-side door. Leaning inside, he opened the temperamental door with a well-aimed thump.

Closing the door behind Laura, he walked around to the driver's side and climbed over the door into his own seat. Backing up to turn the vehicle around, he threw it into gear before heading along a different track to the one Laura had used on her arrival. His pace was a lot more leisurely than that of Toby Oliver.

The whole experience was terribly disconcerting. She was hoping it was because she was still coming to terms with her new surroundings. If she kept telling herself that, then maybe she would believe it. The alternative was not worth considering.

Over the sound of the engine, Marcus told her a bit about Levati as he drove along different dirt tracks that branched off in various directions. He slowed the Land Rover as it neared the village.

"You don't say much, do you?" he commented.

"Depends on the person," she shot back, looking anywhere but at him.

"Look, I'm sorry about yesterday. I was tired. It's a long trip as you well know. I shouldn't have been so hard on you, okay?" He turned the engine off.

She shot him a sideways glance as the Land Rover was surrounded by a throng of children. He turned his attention to the youngsters, greeting them in their native tongue as he climbed out of the vehicle. Crouching down, he was swamped by a sea of brown bodies. He looked up as she carefully straddled the door and jumped down to join him at the front of the car.

Suddenly noticed by the children, she was also swamped by their little figures. He scooped up a little guy of about two, and handed the toddler to her. As the little boy wriggled in her arms she smiled in delight.

"I was beginning to wonder if you could do that," he told her with a smile of his own. A boy of about nine or ten tugged at his sleeve. He bent down to listen.

The boy spoke to Marcus, at the same time pointing at Laura. She saw the doctor laugh and reply, and for some reason she felt embarrassed. Letting the toddler down, she walked beside Marcus as he headed towards the village huts.

"What was that all about?" She wasn't sure if she really wanted to know.

Marcus hesitated. Did he even want to go there? He blew a breath out.

"He said you were very pretty and wanted to know if you were my wife and said it was about time."

"So, did you set him straight?'

He shrugged.

She stopped, pulling him up with her hand on his arm. Marc looked down, shocked at the surge of electricity he felt zap up to his shoulder. He didn't look at her.

"I told him you weren't yet, but I was working on it." Why did he even go there with that comment? He knew it would cause trouble as soon as it was out of his mouth.

CHAPTER FOUR

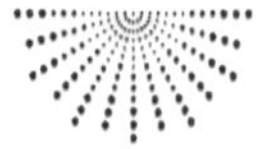

"You said what?" She was incredulous. "How could you?"

Marcus just held his hands up and grinned, not surprised by her reaction. She looked cute when she was steamed up though, so it was worth it. "Well I had to do something to get a rise out of you."

Laura whirled around and marched back to the Land Rover.

He shook his head and ignored her, going instead to speak to some of the village elders. He couldn't help but glance back at the Land Rover from time to time where she sat fuming, with her arms crossed, staring straight ahead.

Sometime later, he made it back to her. "Have you cooled down yet?"

"No."

Sighing inwardly, he climbed back into the Land Rover, farewelling the villagers. The drive back to the hospital was silent. Laura was out of the Land Rover almost before it had stopped next to the staff accommodation block.

"Thanks," she mumbled, and ran lightly up the steps into her quarters.

LAURA SUCCESSFULLY MANAGED to avoid Doctor Bradley for a couple of days. Then, Doctor Reid left.

The next time Laura went into the wards, Doctor Bradley was already there. Mentally she steeled herself as she walked across to where he was already making notes at the end of a patient's bed. "Good morning, Nurse Maxwell. You are a little late this morning. Did you have a bad night?"

"None of your business, Doctor," she muttered quietly before she could help herself. *Oh great, I've given him more ammunition.*

He barely paused in his writing and didn't look up. Handing her the clipboard to return to the end of the bed, he moved on to the next patient as she followed. By the end of the round, she was developing a headache. His bedside manner couldn't be faulted, but he was curt whenever he needed to speak to her. It was a constant battle to keep her mouth in check, when she really wanted to blast him. She was enormously relieved when she could escape to her room.

The whole procedure was repeated over the following few days. She tried to keep up some semblance of normality in the face of the confusion and awkwardness she felt whenever he was around. Laura had no problem talking to and interacting with the other team members. Just Doctor Bradley.

She became a virtual recluse, reluctant to leave the sanctuary of her quarters in case she came across him. Laura knew this wasn't good, but she had no idea what else to do. She just wasn't coping with the doctor in charge.

ABOUT TWO AM one night shift, Laura made her way to the staffroom for a quick cuppa. She was dismayed to find Marcus Bradley in there at that hour of the morning. He had his back to her, busy with some paperwork. With a bit of luck, she could grab her coffee and escape quickly.

No such luck. He was at the door barring her exit before she could reach it.

MARCUS HAD BEEN TRYING to talk to the elusive nurse for days. He didn't want to haul her into his office, but if he didn't get this sorted, he didn't see any other option. Deciding to stake out the staffroom, he'd figured she'd come looking for a coffee shot sometime in the early hours. He had deliberately set himself up away from the door so he wouldn't be so obvious.

His body had been on high alert. He had sensed when she came into the room. Anyone else would have stopped for a chat, but not her.

"Oh no you don't, Nurse. We're going to talk." He took the mug from her hand as she protested, and steered her towards the chair he had just vacated. He sat on the edge of the table facing her. Her long hair, tied in a single plait, hung across her shoulder. He had to resist the urge to reach out and see if her hair was as silky it seemed. He shoved his hands in his pockets to keep them out of harm's way.

"I don't know why you seem to have it in for me, but we can't go around like this for the next couple of months or however long you're supposed to be here. We're a small team and it's important that everyone makes an effort to get along. If you are not willing to work with everyone, and that includes me, then you had better leave on the next plane."

"I'm on duty," she said, getting up.

"Sit down."

SHE DID as she was commanded and focused her attention on the coffee mug in front of her. "We're going to stay here for as long as it takes to get this sorted. Are you going to tell me what the problem is?"

How could she tell him what the problem was when she didn't even know herself? Or did she? He had been playing havoc with her equilibrium ever since she looked up to see him the day he first arrived. She felt like an awkward schoolgirl with her first crush on a boy. Oh no, was that seriously the problem? It couldn't be. Laura closed her eyes and swallowed.

"Laura?"

It was the first time he'd used her name, and she had to admit she liked the way it sounded. She shrugged helplessly before finding a voice. "There's no problem to speak of... nothing I can put my finger on... it's just that... well you... I don't know... something about you rubs me up the wrong way." She heard him get up and walk behind her, pacing, as she shifted uncomfortably in her chair.

"Are you still upset about the day I arrived?"

"No, you were justified to question my capabilities based on my performance that day." Her head turned slightly in his direction, but she kept her eyes to the floor. "I don't know what it is exactly. I'm sorry, that's the best I can come up with."

He was quiet for so long that Laura couldn't help but look around. Standing with his back to her he raked a hand impatiently through his hair and rubbed at his neck. "So, what do you think we can do about it?"

"Keep out of each other's way as much as possible?"

"Or, we could learn to get along with each other."

Laura figured he'd say that. She reached for her coffee with both hands to hold it steady as he came and pulled the chair out next to her, and turned it around. Straddling it, he leant his crossed arms along the top.

"So how did you end up on Levati?"

Okay, it was a straightforward question. Wasn't it?

"I heard Doctor Ogilvie speak at a hospital in Brisbane. He was very… persuasive. I felt like I was in a bit of a rut, so before I quite realised it, I had signed up, arranged my leave, and here I am."

"And?"

"And I'm impressed. The set up here is very good. Much better than Doctor Ogilvie led me to believe."

"Well, Levati is the exception rather than the rule."

"Your family and backers have obviously worked hard to get this place to where it is."

"I'd like to think we have the fundraising formula down, but the truth is, like everyone else, we have to fight for every dollar we get. Sure, we've done well, but there's always so much more we could be doing."

She stood up. "I'm sorry, but I really should get back to work, I'm behind with my patient observations."

He stood and took the coffee mug from her hands. "Go on, I'll see you later." He picked up his own coffee mug and took them over to the sink to rinse. Laura slipped out of the room.

Marcus Bradley was frustrated. Tension among the staff made life difficult in such a close environment. Despite their conversation, Laura Maxwell hadn't changed her stance one bit. She was polite enough, but no more. She wouldn't engage with him, which as doctor-in-charge made working in the confines of the hospital harder than it needed to be. There was nowhere to go to get away. He had to manage staff conflicts on a regular basis, but this one involved him personally. There had to be some way to force the issue. He'd had a few abortive attempts to get her to talk to him but, somehow, she always seemed to neatly sidestep him. She was never around long enough for him to ramp up the charm factor to try and win her over.

Then, he realised the clinic run to the north of the island

would be his best chance to make any inroads. It would be easy enough to volunteer to swap with the rostered doctor. Then all he had to do was orchestrate things so the nurse accompanying him for the trip was Laura Maxwell. Hopefully, spending an enforced day together would help sort things out.

He was in two minds about the whole thing. Despite everything, he had to admit he was attracted to her, and somewhat intrigued. He wanted to get to know her better, but was wary how she would react to the plan.

~

Marcus went looking for Laura after lunch and got straight to the point.

"There's a clinic run tomorrow to the north-east of the island. I need you to come with me."

"It's my day off."

"I know that. I'm sorry."

"Wasn't Kay scheduled to go?" she asked, mentioning one of the other nurses.

"She's not well. It's a long enough trip when you're healthy."

"What about Kylie or Donna?" She was casting around for someone—anyone—else who could go instead.

"They're on duty."

"I'd be happy to work one of their shifts."

"They've already been. It's not an easy trip, and everyone is expected to go at least once."

"I take it you've been more than once."

He shrugged. "I'm used to it now."

"Viv? Elaine?"

He patiently explained why they couldn't go. "Viv is heading home the day after tomorrow, so she needs an easy day. Elaine's on standby. That leaves you, whether you like it or not."

"Not," she muttered to herself. "Wouldn't you prefer someone you'd get on better with?"

His eyes narrowed. "I know the prospect of spending the whole day with me fills you with dread, but you are the only viable option."

Laura dropped her gaze to the ground just in front of her feet. She would just have to suck it up and get over it. "What time do we leave?" she sighed.

"0430. Wear long pants and closed-in shoes, and bring a jacket. It will be cool first up... but by midday... well, you know how hot it gets."

CHAPTER FIVE

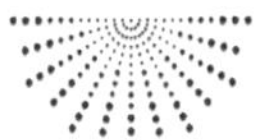

*W*hen the alarm went off, Laura was tempted to roll over and go back to sleep. It should have been her day off and she didn't want to go on the trip, but Doctor Bradley's threat of coming to drag her out of bed if she wasn't ready forced her to get up and moving. After pulling on clothes, she ran a comb through her hair, and quietly exited the building, careful not to let the screen door slam, mindful of others still asleep. The security lighting that flooded the path between the quarters and the hospital enabled her to quickly reach the area where the open-top Land Rover was waiting.

～

MARCUS KEPT GLANCING up as he loaded supplies, wondering if he would have to make good on his promise to wake her up. He kind of hoped he'd need to, wondering what she would be like first thing after waking up. Just as he decided he'd have to go over to her quarters, he saw her walking, head down, towards the Land Rover.

He paused to unashamedly watch her. Her hair was loose and flowing around her shoulders. She wore khaki pants, and a white t-shirt under a navy zip-up jacket that looked good on her. Too good, actually.

Laura raised the back of her hand across her mouth to stifle a yawn as she joined him. He acknowledged her as she grabbed hold of the other side of the tarpaulin and helped haul it over the open back section.

"So, what if it rains?" she asked sleepily.

"If it rains, we get wet." He climbed in, and waited for her to do the same.

The rectangular front windscreen of the obviously ex-army vehicle was divided in two, and a spare tyre was attached to the centre of the bonnet. "Um—so where do you get the Land Rovers from?"

"Not the American military base, if that's what you're wondering. These wheels are British. Came on a slow boat via Singapore."

"Are we going near the Americans today?"

"Not really. They're on the north western end of the island."

He was disappointed when she took a hair tie from her wrist and pulled her hair back, plaiting it as he started the engine and flicked the lights on.

It took a couple of turns before the engine kicked over. Despite being a bit temperamental with old age, the Land Rovers had served them well. They just kept going and going without too much coaxing from the mechanics on the hospital base.

THEY HEADED OFF, into what was for Laura uncharted territory. Doctor Bradley wasn't kidding when he'd said it would be a long, rough trip. All four and a half bone-jarring hours of it. Every part of her body was jolted out of alignment as they crashed into ruts, bounced over potholes and hit the uneven shoulders of the track. The army vehicle wasn't designed for comfort.

The turmoil on the island concerned her, although her companion assured her they were perfectly safe. "You can't go around worrying about the 'what ifs' and 'maybes' in life," he told her. She remained unconvinced.

Marcus allowed them a brief stop after the sun came up. He produced a thermos of coffee and a couple of mugs. Gratefully, she stretched her legs and walked back along the track a short distance.

"I feel like every part of my body is out of place," she confessed when she returned to where he was leaning against the side of the Land Rover. "I'm sure I won't be able to move tomorrow."

There were a few thoughts circling in his head about how she looked fine to him, but he was sure she wouldn't appreciate it if he voiced them out loud. He pushed off the side of the vehicle. "C'mon. Back in. Do you want a hand?"

"I'm not an invalid yet," she answered climbing up. "Doesn't this thing possess any suspension?"

"None that I know of."

She groaned. "I knew it."

ARRIVING at the small settlement sometime after nine, Laura saw there were already people waiting patiently at the wooden hut that would host the make-shift clinic. There was nothing to the building. Just four grey weathered-timber walls and a solid-enough door. Each wall had a window space. Marcus propped the hinged flaps open to let in some… any… breeze.

Once the stored makeshift tables were put out, Laura quickly arrange the supplies. Peeling off her jacket, she got to work, and hardly had time to draw breath again until well after lunch, which she ate on the run. Despite the fact it hadn't taken the two of them long to find a work rhythm, the line-up outside hardly seemed to get any shorter. People had walked a long way to see the doctor.

By late afternoon, Marcus was looking at his watch at regular intervals. He had a growing sense of unease and kept checking their surrounds. What for, exactly, he wasn't sure, but he wanted to be out of there as soon as possible. He didn't want to unduly worry Laura.

"Is there a problem?" she eventually quizzed.

He hesitated, unsure how much to tell her, but honesty was probably the best course of action. "I was hoping to get out of here before sundown. Some of the patients told me there has been rebel activity in the area over the last few nights. I wanted to be as far away as possible by nightfall." He avoided making any eye contact and continued with the bandaging job he was doing.

Laura tried not to show concern as she assisted, but inwardly she was starting to have a bit of a freak-out about their safety. As soon as the last patient was attended to, they quickly packed up.

"That's everything," he said, looking around. "Right, let's go." He gunned the engine and they took off along the trail.

Night quickly closed in around them. Laura reached behind for her jacket as the driver concentrated on the track ahead. Marcus had barely spoken since they'd left, but she could feel the growing tension within him as they drove. Laura scanned the bush around them, looking for anything untoward.

A sudden bang made Laura jump. The Land Rover swerved. Marcus quickly brought it to a halt as they heard the telltale flap-flap of a flat tyre. He swore as he climbed out to investigate.

"There's a torch in the back. You should be able to reach it. It's just behind my seat."

Laura found what Marcus wanted and went around to the other side of the Land Rover where he was crouched down next to the front wheel.

The beam of light shone on the spot briefly and then swung away. "Here, give me some light will you, please?" Marcus didn't get a response.

"Laura."

Still nothing.

He looked up to where she was standing, a look of absolute terror on her face, her free hand clamped over her mouth. He slowly turned to follow her gaze. In the beam from the headlights stood four or five men. All armed. Marcus stood up slowly and took a step toward her while keeping his eyes on the men in front.

"Laura," he said quietly, "don't scream, just stay calm, okay?"

She nodded hesitantly. He reached out, put his hand on her arm and slowly drew her close to his side. She trembled violently. He slipped his arm around her shoulders and held her against him tightly.

His voice echoed in the still of the night as he attempted to elicit a response from the men. There was a short exchange of dialogue.

"They want us to go with them," he told her.

"Did you tell them we're medical personnel?" Laura asked in a strangled whisper.

He replied carefully, in measured tones. "Yes, apparently that's why they put spikes across the track in the first place. The observed us earlier in the day at the clinic and decided to wait for us to leave."

Laura shivered in horror.

"We'll just have to go along and see what they want of us. We don't want to cause any trouble, or they might get angry."

One of the men came to the back of the Land Rover and

pulled at the tarpaulin, looking through the supplies. He seized a couple of the bags and indicated to Marcus that they were to be taken with them. Two were handed to Laura. Marc slipped a backpack on his shoulders and grabbed more bags from the back under the watchful eye of the men.

Cursing himself silently, he walked next to Laura as they were ushered away into the bush.

CHAPTER SIX

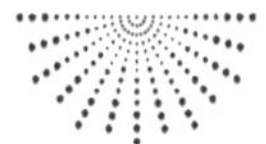

One of the men went on ahead. Two walked directly in front, ever alert, watchful for any sign of trouble, while the other two brought up the rear. It was hard going in the dark of the jungle night.

Laura frequently stumbled over exposed tree roots or other jungle debris. Too terrified to speak, instead she concentrated on each step she took, counting, as her foot made contact with the ground. One, two, three, four. Each time she stumbled she would start over. One, two, three. Anything to take her mind off the countless possibilities that might befall them at any moment, all equally horrid. She refused to dwell on those thoughts, shutting them deliberately out of her mind. Five, six, seven, eight…

Once the moon started to cast its light through the undergrowth, the going became a little easier, but it also served to define their captors more readily. The leader was a tall man, tough and uncompromising, dressed in some sort of military uniform. One could see he was not to be trifled with. The two men directly ahead of Laura were also dressed in camouflage gear that had seen better days. Two boys brought up the rear—for that's what they were, mere boys, maybe sixteen or seventeen, wide-eyed as if this was their first ambush and encounter with hostages. It all seemed new to them and they were uncertain, even hesitant.

The older of the two, from time to time, would make a show of being tough and hit Marcus on the back with the butt of his rifle. At those times the doctor would swear angrily under his breath, but for the most part he was silent, dealing with his own thoughts and personal terrors.

The leader halted the group to check on the prisoners. His gaze travelled over Laura, and she shuddered as she recognised the intent in his eyes. Marcus must have noticed as well, because he took a step closer to her and tried to reassure her. She nodded dumbly at his quietly spoken words as the group fell in again.

TIME LOST all meaning as they trudged along. Marcus estimated they'd been walking for over two hours. Eventually, the jungle parted to reveal a village of sorts. Well, at one point it had been a village, until the rebels no doubt overran it and forced its inhabitants to flee in fear for their very lives.

They stood on the edge of the settlement at the first row of huts. Their leader strode to one of the dwellings and spoke to those inside. Someone emerged and they conferred for a short time, both gesturing towards Laura and Marcus, who were surrounded on all four sides.

Neither of them dared to move or speak up. They waited while their fate was seemingly decided. Soon their chief captor marched over to the group and barked orders. The younger men fell back as the two remaining soldiers led them to a hut a short distance away.

Laura and Marcus were unceremoniously pushed inside the empty hut. Marcus had to duck to get through the doorway. Once inside, he straightened up, dropped the medical bags he was carrying and gratefully shrugged off the weight of the backpack. Taking the other bags from Laura's unresisting fingers, he set them down with the rest. She seemed oblivious as he walked around the confined space.

A guard had been posted at the doorway. Laura sank into a miserable heap on the hard dirt floor. Marcus knelt beside her, rubbing her shoulder without saying anything. Eventually, she sat up and he pulled her against his chest and cradled her there.

SHE CLOSED her eyes and felt his strength infuse her weary body. She almost felt safe from harm. Almost.

"How are you going?" he asked quietly, his voice close to her ear.

"I don't know. I'm not brave enough to think about it too much. I'd prefer not to look too closely." She pulled herself gently out of his arms, reluctant to leave the warmth and strength she felt. "So, what so we do now?"

Marcus shrugged helplessly. "Nothing we can do, except wait and see what happens."

"Do you think they mean to hurt us?" She gulped.

Marcus considered her question for a while. "I don't think so." He shook his head slowly. "They've already had ample time to do that. I'm hoping they're more interested in our medical expertise."

"You mean treating their sick and wounded?"

He nodded. "Laura, I'm sorry I got you into this mess."

She took his hands into her own. "You couldn't have done anything to stop it."

"I know, but I still feel responsible."

"Well, don't." She squeezed his hands, then embarrassment engulfed her as she realised what she was doing. Grateful the darkened interior of the hut wouldn't betray her flushed features, she let go of his hands. Despite the jacket she wore, the cool night air finally reached her. "I'm getting cold all of a sudden."

"Funny, I thought I was starting to warm up, myself."

Scrambling to her feet she cast her eyes around their prison. "There's some sort of woven mat in the corner. Maybe that's a bed?"

"Go for it."

"What about you."

"I'll be fine. Go on, see if you can get some sleep."

Laura did as she was told. Uncomfortable was an understatement. She lay with her eyes closed. The cold began to seep into her bones, into her very soul it seemed, from the bare dirt floor.

"Marcus?"

"I'm just here." His voice sounded off to her left.

"I don't like being by myself. Would you mind coming a bit closer?" He obliged, sitting next to where she had stretched out. She shivered.

"Still cold hey?"

Her voice was very small. "Yes."

"Like me to help keep you warm?"

She agreed before she could even think about it.

"Thought you'd never ask," he told her as he slipped down beside her. "How's that?"

"No, closer." He pressed himself against the length of her body and wrapped his arm around her.

"Better?" he whispered in her ear.

"Mmmm, much." Then she added, "Don't go getting any ideas, Doctor. This is strictly to prevent hypothermia."

"Absolutely," he agreed.

MARCUS HARDLY THOUGHT hypothermia was going to be a problem in the tropics. Shock was probably the likely cause of her feeling cold. But he wasn't going to argue if it meant he could hold her like this.

Soon, he felt her relax against his body and heard the pattern of her breathing change as she fell asleep. The floral smell of her shampoo reached him, along with the sweat from the long day —not that he minded in the least. Her hand lay across his arm and her touch, even in her sleep, sent tingling clear up to his shoulder. She wriggled and he pulled her up against his chest, closer. A tiny sigh escaped her. He couldn't stop himself from planting a soft kiss on the side of her neck.

This was something he could get used to, he thought, as he finally drifted fitfully off to sleep.

EVERY BONE in her body seemed to ache when Laura woke next morning. The realisation of their predicament flooded back in the first few seconds after she opened her eyes and saw the thatched roof above her. Stretching gingerly, she propped herself up on her elbows.

Marcus sat on the floor with his back against the adjoining woven bamboo wall, watching her. "Morning. How did you sleep?"

"Not very well. I have the bruises to prove it."

"Breakfast is served, madam." He indicated something unidentifiable next to him.

"What is it?"

"Hot buttered croissants, your choice of cereals, fresh fruit with yoghurt, and coffee or tea to finish."

Laura groaned and lay back. "What is it really?"

"I'm not sure, but it seems edible… and there's some water as well."

Laura rolled over and got to her feet to join him.

"Edible, but not very tasty." She forced the food down with help from the water. "What shall we do next?" she asked as she wiped her mouth on her jacket sleeve. "Swimming? Water skiing? What about parasailing? I've always wanted to try that." The banter served to distract them from their dismal surroundings.

"You choose."

"How about we escape?" He shook his head, standing in the confined space. "You could overpower the guard and we could slip away into the jungle."

"Laura, there's more than one of them and they'd know the area well. I don't have any idea where we are. They'd track us down quickly and we could be worse off. You've seen too many movies."

She scrambled up to stand next to him. "You seem to speak the language. I've heard you can charm your way around anyone. Why don't you talk your way out?"

He raised an eyebrow at her. "Who have you been talking to?"

"Angela Reid seems to rate your ability to charm pretty highly."

"It doesn't appear to have worked on you."

"You win some, you lose some." She shrugged, trying to appear bored with the whole concept.

"Maybe I should try harder," came the suggestion.

"Maybe you shouldn't waste your breath, Doctor Bradley." She crossed her arms and stood glaring at him defiantly.

Marcus made an assessing gaze. "Still don't like me much, do you?"

When she declined to comment, he continued, "I suggest we call a truce and cease all hostilities until we get out of this place. It won't help matters if we're at each other constantly."

"Might relieve the boredom."

He ignored her and crossed to where the medical supplies had been dumped the previous night. Crouching down, he flipped the catch and opened the first lid. "I wasn't sure in the dark which ones we grabbed."

Laura watched as he inspected the contents and then set the container aside. He repeated the process with the next. Laura relaxed her stance. "I don't suppose there'd be any things like, you know, toilet paper or any other such luxuries?" Marcus reached for the third case and unzipped it. Silently he handed her what she'd asked for. She got down next to him clutching the roll of toilet paper. "What other goodies are in there?" He let her take a look.

"I always keep a grab bag of emergency type stuff…"

"There's even soap." She reached for it. "I could go for a shower. Pity there's no water." She sighed.

Marcus held his hand up. Laura quietened.

"Can you hear that?"

"No, what exactly?"

"Sounds like a helicopter."

Their eyes automatically looked to the hut roof as if they could see beyond it, above the jungle canopy. Was their rescue imminent?

The whirl of the blades grew louder, but they dared not venture outside to attract attention.

We're here! We're here! Laura chanted under her breath as the helicopter circled the area before disappearing again.

No, don't leave us! She despaired, covering her face with her hands.

Marcus grabbed her arm. "It's only a matter of time before we are rescued."

Over the next couple of days, the helicopter returned, circling the area. Each time, they got their hopes up. Then nothing.

A MOVEMENT outside the hut attracted her attention. Time for a change of guards. The hut where they were being held was away from the others, so they never saw another human apart from their guard. They were not allowed outside, except to answer the call of nature at a discreet distance from the hut. Laura learned to be quick. Besides the possibility of encountering any nasties in the jungle growth, she didn't want to earn the wrath of the guards, who would come looking for her if she was too long.

Food arrived twice a day. Even if they weren't sure what they were eating, they weren't totally starving.

Marcus had somehow managed to get hold of a container of water into which he added purification tablets from their supplies, making it relatively safe to drink.

The days were hot and sticky and the nights, thankfully, cooler. Their sleeping time was governed by the sun as they had no access to artificial lighting. Laura felt uncomfortable about sharing with Marcus the miserable amount of bedding they'd been given, which amounted to no more than a threadbare blanket, but at the same time she felt safer with his presence alongside her. Inching as far away from him in the dark as she dared, she would wait until his breathing indicated he was asleep before she relaxed and eventually did likewise. Inevitably, in the morning, she would find herself curled up against him with his arms around her.

Marcus never made any comment and just seemed to accept their sleeping arrangements as something necessary for their survival. She was both relieved and puzzled that he never tried to take advantage of the situation they found themselves in. She pushed her embarrassment away and locked it up with as many of her other emotions as she could gather.

THERE WASN'T MUCH they could do in the hut except talk. Marcus found some notepaper and a pen in one of the bags and wrote out topics on small torn pieces. Every day they chose one and used it as the theme. Despite Laura's initial reluctance, Marcus was able to get her to open up, and they had spirited debate on a huge range of issues from music and movies to politics and social issues. Marcus, as she already knew, was a good conversationalist, and she doubted her ability to make a worthwhile contribution to any discussion—but she found him easy to talk to and was soon able to hold her own in any argument. He often teased and baited to get a rise out of her. Laura quickly learned to give as good as she got and enjoyed the repartee.

Laura held the container while Marcus took out a slip of paper.

"Looks like today we are talking about ourselves and our families," he announced. "Okay, you go first."

"Name: Laura Catherine Maxwell. Age: thirty-two. Born September eighth to John and Catherine Maxwell. Only child. My mother died when I was in senior at high school. Dad eventually remarried. Her name is Brooke and they have Keith, eleven, Jeffrey, nine, and baby Chloe is about eight months. I don't see them all that often. Brooke and I don't get on that well. I was living with them when the boys were younger. I was a free babysitting service-slash-housekeeper and so on. Eventually I moved across town. My dad is approaching sixty and Brooke is forty-one."

She answered the questions Marcus asked about her school life before quizzing him about his own family. She already knew his father's reputation as a top specialist and that his older brother was a lawyer. She learned Stephen was thirty-eight, two years older than Marcus. Married to Danielle. They had twin daughters, Ashlee and Jacinta, aged seven. Their son Luke was nine and a half. "My mother, Emma, was a GP. She and my dad met at med school. She died of cancer five years ago." He sounded wistful.

"Still miss her, huh?"

"Yep. She and dad were happily married for thirty-five years."

She glanced over at him, but he was somewhere miles away.

"I hope when I finally get married, my partnership will be as happy and successful as theirs was," he said.

"I'm surprised someone hasn't snapped you up long before now."

MARCUS FELT SUDDENLY RESTLESS. He got up from where he'd been sitting and stretched, then walked around while Laura sat hugging her knees to her chest. He blew a breath out, wondering just what to say.

"Came close a couple of times," he admitted. "But it's such a big step to take. When you've got such a high standard to look up to, you tend to be a bit particular about choosing a life partner. Of course, being married to my work doesn't help much either." They were both silent for a while. So, what was her story? "What about you, Laura?" He looked over at her as she hugged her knees tighter and took a deep breath before answering. He wondered if she had been married at one time.

"Unlike you, my parents' marriage wasn't all that wonderful. It was probably a blessing that my mother died. So, I guess I've shied away from wanting to make a commitment, and, as you said, being married to your job doesn't help."

THANKFULLY FOR LAURA, the conversation drifted to schooling and university life. They laughed at some of their anecdotes of growing up. Marcus was a born raconteur. It was easy to forget, if just for a little while, the environment around them. They were just two people getting to know each other.

CHAPTER SEVEN

Sometime after midnight, Laura was woken by an explosion and the sound of gunfire. "What on earth—?"

Marcus cut her off as he crawled over to the doorway. There was a lot of shouting and angry voices. After what seemed like an eternity, he crept back to where she was huddled in the corner.

"As far as I can tell, our friends have gone on a drinking binge. There's a bit of a fight going on around the campfire."

Laura shivered. Marcus reached for her and put a comforting arm around her shoulder.

The noises grew louder and louder. Laura cowered in the corner as the men got closer to their hut. A scuffle broke out near the doorway. She could just make out what she thought were fists swinging. The guard connected with one of the drunks. Suddenly a gun was drawn.

Laura gasped and Marcus clapped his hand across her mouth, motioning her to keep quiet. The drunks argued with the guard, gesticulating wildly towards the inside of the hut. The guard stood his ground and after a lot of discussion, the men went back to the distant campfire. She felt Marcus relax and he dropped his hand.

"What did they want?" she asked him hesitantly. He was shaking his head. "Marcus?"

He let out a sharp breath. "They wanted you."

Laura's strangled sob was heartbreaking and he gathered her against his chest. The tears flowed silently and unchecked. Initially he had thought it best to be completely honest with her. But now he wasn't so sure as he stroked her hair and murmured words of comfort.

It was the first time since their capture she'd given way to tears. He cursed himself silently again for getting them into this predicament. Sleep was banished as the drunken revelry continued. Fearful of a return visit, he sat beside her, straining to hear in case footsteps approached.

EVENTUALLY, as dawn streaked the sky, Laura fell into an uneasy sleep, but was chased through her dreams by drunken rebels. The faceless men pursued her through the jungle. She could hear them gaining as she stumbled and tripped in a frantic attempt to evade capture. Night sounds of the jungle terrorised her as she fought blindly through the undergrowth. They were gaining on her. They wanted her. She must not be caught.

Suddenly they were all around her. Leering. Groping. One grabbed her by the arm. Wildly she struggled as his grip tightened.

"Laura, Laura." Marc's voice finally reached into her subconscious and pulled her out of her nightmare. He soothed her wild-eyed fear as she surfaced from the dark recesses of her mind. She lay on her back for a long while, staring at the thatched roof of the hut as she tried to right her world. The vivid pictures haunted her even now.

Laura covered her face with her arm, sucking in large gulps

of air. The images and the emotions they evoked would not be easily banished. Slowly, she became aware of her surroundings.

Marcus was moving around quietly. He tucked an arm under her and helped her sit up, then encouraged her to try and eat something.

BOTH HEARD the noise at the entrance of the hut at the same time. Marc went forward to speak to the men, while she pressed herself against the back corner.

"A few people got hurt last night," he told her when he returned a short time later. "They want us to patch them up."

"No way!" she spat out.

Marcus crouched down next to her. "Look, I know the idea is repulsive, but we can't afford to antagonise them if we want to get out of here alive."

"I can't, Marcus."

He took her hands gently. "Laura, they were drunk last night. Likely as not they won't remember anything about their threats."

She didn't want to be convinced, but when she looked into his eyes, she knew she couldn't refuse. "Okay," she mumbled, her nod barely perceptible.

"Good girl." He went to retrieve the supplies. She slipped her jacket on despite the warm day, and zipped it up. "They're bringing them down here. We'll treat them outside." The guard stood back as they emerged, blinking, into the brightness of the morning sun.

THE WALKING WOUNDED ARRIVED within minutes. Marcus directed them to sit wherever they could in the shade of the nearby trees. Laura followed him from patient to patient. Most were suffering gashes, probably from broken glass. He was kept busy stitching wounds while keeping a watch on Laura out of the corner of his eye.

~

SHE FROZE. The blood drained away from every part of her body as she recognised the voice of the man who had drunkenly argued with their guard the night before.

Marcus spoke calmly as she tried to get her emotions in check. Shaking visibly, she handed him what he'd asked for.

As he reached out with one hand to take the swab, the other grasped her hand firmly. She looked up at him and was able to draw strength and reassurance from his unwavering gaze.

Their patient spoke rapidly to the doctor. Marcus listened and responded with barely controlled anger. The rebel looked from her to Marcus and back, then shrugged. Marcus kept working and talking quietly to Laura as he did so.

"Our friend here was making some unwelcome suggestions towards you. I told him you were my wife and if he so much as lays a finger on you, I will kill him."

Laura had to turn away. Tears tried to force their way from her eyes. The protective stance he'd taken touched her more than she would have expected.

Soon after the last person had been attended to, four men struggled back with a large, battered metal container strung somehow between two poles. Water slopped over the sides as they set it down. Then they were alone again except for their guard.

Marcus wasted no time. He grabbed the bar of soap and stripped off to his waist. Kneeling at the water container he quickly splashed himself and washed off, then dunked his shirt into the water and proceeded to clean it.

Laura took herself into the hut and quickly removed her t-shirt and underwear. She slipped her jacket back on and was just refastening her long pants when Marcus entered, still wet.

~

HE PAUSED BRIEFLY in the doorway. He'd been trying to come up with something that would lighten the mood and give her something else to think about. He spied the small pile on the floor and scooped them up. "Want me to wash your clothes?" He held up the soap.

"No thanks, I'll manage." She snatched the soap and took the clothes back.

A tree branch at the side of the hut became a makeshift line as she draped her underwear over it. At least they would be a little fresher. Later, she repeated the process with her long pants, borrowing Marc's shirt, which covered her like a dress, for the duration. Rolling the sleeves up, she laced up her shoes before going out to the wash tub. Her hair was annoying her, and she dearly would have loved to wash it, but she had no way of combing out the tangles. Instead she twisted the plait up and fashioned a bun of sorts.

Laura ignored Marcus as he came to stand near her. Despite the heat, Laura could feel the colour rising in her face.

"You know," he teased, giving her a cheeky grin, "seeing as how we're married and everything, I think it would be worthwhile to put on a bit of a show for our jailer over there in case he's not convinced."

Before Laura had time to protest, he'd pulled her into his arms and claimed her lips. Initially she was too shocked to react. Then her hands went to his chest to push him away. Well that's what she intended, but as he deepened the kiss, her arms somehow found their way up to entwine themselves around his neck.

The stubble on his face—unshaven for twelve days—was rough, but not abrasive. Laura forgot where she was as she closed her eyes and savoured the faint aroma of the soap that clung to him. As much as she wanted to deny all that was going on, the feelings he was arousing deep within her very being pressed her tighter against his powerful frame. A hunger exploded within her as his mouth marauded hers.

~

SURFACING, Marcus stopped to take in her dazed features. He ran his thumb gently across her lips and around her cheek. If he was completely honest, kissing her was something he had wanted to do for a while. His eyes latched onto hers and her breath caught. He wanted to dive right into their rich depth.

~

THE AMUSED LAUGH of the watching guard brought Laura to her senses. Embarrassment quickly overtook passion, and she turned her face away.

She wrenched herself out of Marcus's grasp and stalked off to the hut. Her hands trembled as she fought to steady her breathing. She walked around the inside of the hut, too worked up to sit. Those kisses had such an effect on her. For good or bad, she couldn't tell. Whatever it was, it threatened to totally overwhelm her.

Soon after, Marc strolled in as if nothing had happened. She tried not to take any notice of him. But she was on heightened alert for every move he made. Then he got too close.

"Keep away from me," she warned.

"Why?" he queried. "You enjoyed it just as much as I did."

She shook her head, not daring to look at him in case he saw the truth in her eyes.

"We are..."—she struggled to get words out in a coherent form—"both... emotionally vulnerable at the moment. None of this would have happened in the real world."

"You don't know that."

"No, I'm sure of it. This situation…"—she gestured around her—"is so different. We're doing things that we wouldn't in normal circumstances. Everything will be totally different when we are away from here."

"If pretending to be married is going to help keep you from being raped by those animals out there, then I think a public display of affection is worth it. I promise I won't make a move without telling you first, which is unlikely from them."

Okay, when he put it like that. "It doesn't seem like I have much choice," she said slowly.

"I assure you it won't be any hardship for me."

Laura shot him a killing glance, but he was busy checking through his medical supply bags.

He had to move away from her. The pull to reach for her again was getting stronger and he needed to put some distance between them, however small, to try to regain his composure. Going through the medical supplies was the only thing Marcus could think of to occupy his hands. Sorting and checking. Checking and sorting. He already knew the contents of each bag off by heart, but he went through each bag carefully, as if he was seeing them for the first time.

CHAPTER EIGHT

*D*ay Eighteen. The length of their confinement was beginning to take its toll. Both had lost a lot of weight.

Night had become Laura's enemy. She struggled with recurring nightmares as rebels chased her unrelentingly through the jungle. She knew her companion was keeping a careful eye on her, concerned for her well-being.

The monotony of their existence was rapidly becoming a major hurdle to overcome. By now, they knew almost all there was to know about each other. Marcus had found a spiral-bound notebook and was keeping a diligent record of their time as prisoners.

"Maybe it will form the basis of a best seller one day," he told her when she questioned him.

"Why bother, we're never getting out of here," she replied despondently.

"You can't give up, Laura."

"Why not? It seems the outside world has. Nobody knows where we are. Nobody is doing anything about it."

"Never let go of your hope, Laura. You have to believe we

will get out of here soon. Every day is another day closer to freedom."

She grumbled to herself and went to sit just outside the hut. They knew their guards quite well by now. Which ones were more lenient and allowed them outside for some—albeit limited —exercise. A couple were even conciliatory, but Laura remained wary and never ventured off without her "husband".

THE NOISE of distant gunfire pulled Marcus out of his sleep. Laura was already awake next to him; he could just make her out, staring up at the blackness of the hut's roof. He reached out and found her hand, and gave what he hoped was a reassuring squeeze. She rolled away from him, but not before he caught the look of fear on her face. He moved closer to her and wrapped his arm around her as he brought his body into contact with hers. She stiffened for what seemed a long time and then he gradually felt her relax, a little.

They were both wide awake and unable to sleep for what seemed like a long time. Waiting for the noise to abate.

He wasn't sure exactly when he eventually fell asleep.

IN THE EARLY MORNING LIGHT, they were summonsed to attend a shooting victim. Marcus gathered the meagre medical supplies together, and they were led under guard to one of the huts in the main village area. There was a clearing in the middle of the village, surrounded on all sides by native dwellings. A path entered the main part of the village at one end and continued out on the opposite side.

The hut they were directed to had furniture of sorts inside. A couple of crudely made chairs, a rough bench that served as storage. Marcus automatically went to the bed in the corner.

Leaning over the patient he uncovered the shoulder wound and swore softly. "This is nasty… He must be all of sixteen or seventeen."

"Can you do anything for him?" she asked, coming up to stand beside him.

"I can only try. He's burning up. There's already an infection. Who knows how long he's been carrying this? My guess is he was trying to fight on. It won't be easy in these conditions. But I don't want to think of the consequences if we fail."

He cleared the bench and Laura helped him set out the limited amount of equipment. Drawing in a deep breath to sustain himself, he bent to his task. He made a request for help to restrain the patient, acutely aware of Laura as she stood by his elbow, watching and responding to his requests. They had to improvise as they went along, and he couldn't help being impressed by her manner under duress.

Finally, he stood upright again. "Well, that's done, now we have to wait and see. Thanks for your help."

THEY EACH TOOK it in turns to monitor the patient while the other tried to rest. It was touch and go for many hours. Marcus could only administer what drugs he had, and they weren't much. A couple of old hurricane lamps were brought to them as night fell. Laura wrung out bits of torn cloth in a beat-up metal container of water, attempting to reduce the fever.

She dozed intermittently, and started as the boy stirred. She checked his temperature; the fever had broken. Finally.

The boy was awake. Gently, she roused Marcus. His eyes flew open, and once he realised what was going on, he went to the bedside. He murmured a few words in the boy's language and listened to his groggy reply.

"I think we've done it," he told her simply. He held up his hand for a high five, then gave Laura a quick hug.

"Great work, Doctor." She grinned at him tiredly.

"Yeah well, I couldn't have done it without you, Nurse." He spent a lengthy amount of time relaying instructions about the care of the patient to others who could help look after the young man, ensuring they were fully understood.

With their guard, he and Laura walked the length of the village back to their prison hut. Exhausted, they slumped down. Eventually, they both managed to fall into a restless sleep.

A DAY LATER, just as they were about to return for yet another check on the patient, they were surprised to hear a voice asking for them in English outside their hut. Curious, Marcus went to the door.

Laura strained to listen in.

"You are the doctor who saved my son?"

"If you mean the youngster at the other end of the village who was shot, then yes, my nurse and I saved his life."

"I am so grateful," the voice answered. The accent was heavy and clipped. "He is my youngest son. He fights like his father, General Malatinu. But I must say thank you to your nurse as well. Bring her out."

"I'll just go and get *my wife*."

Laura was already on her feet when Marcus reached her. He put a finger to his lips in a signal for her to keep her quiet, then silently pulled the signet ring off his finger. With his back blocking the view from the hut entrance, he reached for her left hand and slid it onto her ring finger. Taking her hand firmly in his, he took her to the general.

Marcus stood head and shoulders above the other man, who was thickset with a small moustache. A scar ran across his right cheek and disappeared around behind his ear. Dressed in military fatigues, he looked quite fierce. Laura would've taken a step back except that Marcus was right behind her.

"This is my wife," he said firmly. "She helped me operate on your son."

Laura was surprised when the general clicked his heels and bowed. When he reached to grasp her hand, Marcus tapped her left arm lightly so she would extend it. The general took her slender hand in his two dark ones and kissed the top of it. The sun glinted on Marc's signet ring as Laura dropped her hand.

"All the men here have been telling me how beautiful you are. I envy you, Doctor; you are a lucky man."

Marcus nodded as he slipped an arm around her shoulders.

"Is there anything I can get you?"

"Actually," Marcus replied coolly, "we'd both like to be released so we can go home."

"No, it is not possible." The general was adamant.

"But we saved your son's life."

"We need you to care for our wounded."

"Our supplies are almost exhausted; we can't be of much help without medication and other supplies."

"We will get some more for you. You must stay." The general turned on his heel and marched away. Laura sagged against Marc in despair.

"We'll never get out of here."

"Remember what I said, don't give up." He kissed the top of her head. "We'll find a way out."

LAURA HAD no idea how long they had been driving. Both she and Marcus had been blindfolded and bundled into a Jeep in the early hours of the morning. As strange as it seemed, she was not scared. Marc's firm grip on her hand helped, but still, she was surprised at her apparent calm.

They were flung forward as the vehicle came to a sudden stop. There was movement around her. Their captors helped them out and made them stand together. Marcus translated what he was being told. "We're being released, but we're not allowed to remove the blindfolds until they are gone." The engine revved and the rebels took off.

As soon as the sound of the vehicle could no longer be heard, Marcus ripped off his blindfold and untied Laura's.

She blinked in the early morning sun. "Why do you think the general changed his mind?"

"Who knows? Guilt perhaps. A gesture of goodwill for saving his son. Maybe I appealed to his better nature. He obviously has one after all. I'm not going to question it. Just grateful to be out of there."

Marc scouted around. "I think we might be near the military base." He led the way along the track until they came to a fork. He checked their surrounds carefully.

"This way." He indicated the left-hand track, making sure she was following behind him as they walked in silence. They were free, but how safe were they really?

THE SUN ROSE HIGHER and they grew increasingly hot, but there was no water to quench their thirst. How much longer would they have to walk. Could they walk much further?

Laura would've stumbled into the electric fence if Marcus hadn't pulled her back in the nick of time. "It's the perimeter of the military base," he told her. They followed the treed fence line for a very long time until finally there was an entrance. The lone sentry was startled to see them appear out of nowhere.

Marcus was quick to introduce them. "I'm Doctor Marcus Bradley and this is Nurse Laura Maxwell. We work for the Medi-Aid organisation."

The light of recognition dawned in the soldier's eyes. "Hey, you're those two Australian aid workers that got kidnapped, aren't you?"

Marcus nodded.

"Man, we've been helping to look for you guys, but we figured they might have killed you. Did they let you go?"

Marcus nodded again.

"Far out."

"Would you have any water by any chance? We haven't had any for a long time and we're parched."

"Oh yeah." The soldier twisted around, grabbed a drink canteen and handed it over.

Laura almost snatched it out of the guy's hand. She unscrewed the lid and took a few mouthfuls before reluctantly handing it over to her companion.

The guard was keen to talk and Marcus let him ramble on for a while before suggesting that he should call for someone to come and get them.

"Sure thing. Man, I can't believe you guys are alive." The young soldier made a call and within minutes a Jeep arrived to collect them.

Their driver also talked nonstop on the short trip to the main compound. It seemed that almost everyone at the base had spent some time searching for them at the request of the Australian government. They followed the sergeant into one of the buildings.

Finally, after twenty-two days, thirteen hours and forty-seven minutes, they were safe.

CHAPTER NINE

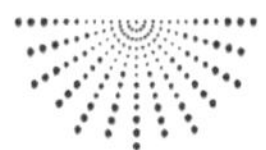

 fter so many days of inactivity, things seemed to Laura to be moving rapidly.

They were allowed to have their first real meal and Laura blissfully devoured each morsel on the plate in front of her, reminding herself to eat slowly.

The base doctor was keen to give them a thorough once-over, but Laura begged to be allowed a shower first, which was duly arranged. With the instruction that she could take as long as she wanted, Laura revelled in the longest shower of her life. Allowing the warm water to sluice over her body until the heat petered out, she scrubbed her skin until it felt clean again. Combing her hair out was an effort, but she was determined to get it untangled. Her head felt so much lighter when she finally emerged from the shower. After towelling off she was thrilled to be able to sit and brush her hair. One of the female officers was kind enough to lend her a spare uniform. She never wanted to see the other clothes again.

Leaving her hair hanging loose, she followed her escort to the doctor's room. Marcus had just finished. Clean shaven and also dressed in military clothes, he was already looking much better. But Laura realised it would take some time before they both recovered physically from the ordeal of the last three weeks. Mentally? Well, who would know?

The doctor, however, was pleased. "Considering all you've been through, you're in pretty good shape."

"Thanks, Doc." Laura got down off the examination table.

"I've recommended to Marcus that you take some multi-vitamins to help boost your immune system. I'll give you a list of some other supplements you should think about taking for a while. I know you probably don't want to hear this, but you should take things easy for a while."

Laura rolled her eyes. "I've been taking it easy for three weeks." She sat down on the chair next to the doctor's desk as he wrote on a notepad for her and tore off the sheet, handing it to her.

"Nevertheless, I think you should ease yourself back into life again."

Laura nodded.

The doctor went on, "Marcus told me he's concerned that you've been having nightmares on a regular basis."

Laura felt the colour drain from her face. She'd been afraid he'd mention that. "There was an incident that seemed to trigger some bad dreams," she admitted, slowly.

"Hmm, so Marcus said. Do you want me to organise for you to see a—"

"No, not at this stage," she broke in hastily. "I'd like to see how I go now I'm away from there."

The doctor seemed doubtful. "Promise me you will get some professional help if the nightmares continue."

Laura agreed, so he would drop the subject.

At the debriefing, they discovered how many personnel had been out looking for them in the first few days they had gone missing. Even though the authorities had scaled back after ten days, there was still an active search in progress.

Marcus let them know a helicopter had flown over their location, more than once.

~

LAURA WASN'T SURPRISED to find Doctor Bradley the centre of attention in the officers' mess that evening. Although he moved over to make room for her to join him, and included her in the conversation, Laura felt she had become all but invisible.

In the real world, Marcus Bradley hardly knew she existed. He did, however, walk her to her room later that night. She paused before going in, struggling with thoughts she could barely comprehend, let alone express to the man next to her.

"You sure you're going to be able to sleep without me?" he teased.

"Quite sure, Doctor Bradley."

"I'm just down the corridor to the left, if you change your mind."

"I'll keep your offer in mind." She pushed at his chest lightly. "Go on, you."

~

MARCUS SAW HER SMILE, but it didn't reach her eyes. He put a finger under her chin to lift her face up to his. "Laura, are you okay?" She looked tired and more than a little overwhelmed.

"I guess getting back to civilisation might be harder than I thought."

"You'll get there," he told her, brushing a finger against her cheek. "One thing I noticed over the last couple of weeks was your inner strength and capacity to cope with all that was thrown at you. A lot of others would have gone to pieces."

Laura shrugged. "I wouldn't have made it without you to get me through."

He shook his head. "I think you are selling yourself way too short, Nurse Maxwell."

She sighed.

He couldn't help himself and bent his head to brush her lips fleetingly with his own. "Goodnight, Laura. I hope you can sleep well."

"So do I, Marcus."

~

SHE DIDN'T. As soon as her head hit the pillow, the memories of her time in captivity overwhelmed her as they fought to gain control of her mind. Despite the comfort of being in a real bed again, Laura tossed and turned, unable to find any relief until, at last, she fell into an exhausted, haunted sleep.

Early next morning, Laura wandered aimlessly. Unsure of herself and unable to sleep any longer, she dressed and escaped the confines of the small room. Fresh air. But she didn't take in any of her surrounds. The base personnel were friendly, although they kept their distance, allowing her time to herself.

Trying to come to terms with this island and all that she had been through was something she could not even begin to understand. Totally lost in thought, she headed back to the main building and walked around a corner only to collide with Marcus.

He automatically reached out to steady her. "Hey, careful there, Nurse Maxwell."

"Sorry, Marc, I guess I should have been paying more attention."

He dropped his arms as she stepped back. "Have you had breakfast yet?"

"No, I've been out walking," she told Marcus, taking in his army-issue uniform and his sleep tousled hair. "Late night huh?"

"Yeah, well, I must admit I did spend a few hours talking with the doctor. Well, I talked mostly, and he listened." Marcus walked beside her to the officers' mess. "It was good to be able to talk things through with another doctor."

"Did it help?" Laura wanted to know.

"I think it will be a lengthy, ongoing process, but yes, it

helped to be able to start to put things in some sort of perspective."

She was pleased for him.

"How did you sleep, Laura?"

She shook her head as they walked into the almost deserted room.

Any further conversation was halted as the head chef came over to greet them. The kitchen staff had gone all out to entice them. She needed no second bidding to indulge in the fresh food that arrived, along with the endless coffee supply. Laura ate more this time around, but she was being cautious considering the little they had eaten over the last few weeks. Marcus received a message to go speak to the commanding officer, and he promised to catch up with her later.

A couple of young off-duty officers took it upon themselves to show her around. She was happy to oblige them, and listened to them rattle off facts and figures about the base.

After a while, an intense longing for another shower led her to excuse herself to her guides. Explaining that she would like to rest, she scurried back to her room.

Adjusting the spray of water to the right temperature, Laura was quick to get under the shower to enjoy the warm stream as it soothed and relaxed her. She knew she shouldn't take so long, but it felt so wonderful and she washed her hair again. The smell of the shampoo was a delight to her jaded senses, and she repeated the process a couple more times. It was so good to be clean again. Finally, feeling guilty, she reluctantly turned off the water supply and towelled dry.

MARC FOUND his way to Laura's room. He had a proposition for her but was wary how she would react. He realised once they got back to Australia, they would probably go their separate ways. Keen to keep her in his life for a bit longer, it seemed he may have found a way to do that, at least for the short term.

She was quick to answer his knock. There was a towel around her hair. Obviously, she had been in the shower, again. Maybe it was part of her coping mechanism. The white t-shirt she was wearing and the very short running shorts proved to be a huge distraction. Thankfully, she turned and walked across the room before he gave in to his sudden urge to pull her into his arms and— Never mind.

He closed his eyes briefly and took a deep breath to pull himself together. "Sorry to intrude, but we need to talk."

"About what?"

"You had better sit down." He gestured to the end of the bed as he took the chair by the small desk.

Unwrapping her hair, she let it fall in a tangled mess around her as she sat on the end of the bed. Tugging at it, she commented ruefully, "After the last few weeks, I'm giving serious consideration to getting this cut off, maybe to here." She indicated a spot high on her neck.

"That's a bit premature. You have lovely hair—why don't you see how it responds to treatment when you get back home?"

She was apparently taken aback by the compliment. "Humpf. It's not so lovely at the moment. It will at least need a good trim." She pulled it back into some semblance of order as she waited for Marcus to discuss what he came to talk about.

"The base has been inundated with calls from the media about us." Laura looked surprised as he went on, "Apparently, we've caused bit of a stir back home… well, actually, not just back home. The international media have picked up on it as well."

"Picked up on what?"

"The story… our story, being kidnapped and such. It could mean a lot of publicity for Medi-Aid."

"That's good, isn't it?" she admitted.

He'd hoped she would respond like that. Now for the next part.

"Well, it's only the start. One of the big women's magazines is offering a substantial amount of money to do an exclusive story and photo spread. It would be linked to a range of television shows from the same organisation."

Laura looked at her hands as she tried to take in what he was saying. "You'd use the money for Medi-Aid no doubt. It would be a wonderful opportunity for you, Marcus, to raise the profile of Medi-Aid and promote your work, and raise some funds as well." She looked up at him. "I think you should do it."

Now for the kicker, he thought. *Here goes.*

"Laura," he said gently, "I don't think you fully understand. It's a women's magazine—they're interested in the romance aspect of our capture."

"There is no romance."

"I know, but they found out about the ring thing and want to follow up on that idea."

Laura dropped her eyes to the signet ring she was still wearing. "All I want to do," she said firmly, "is to go home and get my life back together. I didn't ask for any publicity and I don't want any."

He pushed a hand back through his hair. "Look, I know how you feel. I have no idea how they found out, but they'll more than double the money if we are both involved."

"No."

"You said yourself it would be a good opportunity. The money would certainly go a long way to helping in places like Levati." He could tell by her expression she was softening to the idea.

"What would I have to do?"

"Pretend we are engaged."

Her "no" was adamant. He wasn't surprised by her reaction —it was the same one he'd felt when he took the call. It would be a huge thing to pull off. The whole idea had chased itself around in his head for a long time. Could they do it? Should they do it? Maybe he should've set the magazine rep straight from the start. That had been his intention, until the amount of money had been mentioned.

"Hear me out. It would only be until the publicity dies a natural death, say four to six months, and then we can go our separate ways."

"What if they find out?"

He scrambled to come up with something. "We'll just tell them the media scrutiny was too much… What was it you said? We were emotionally vulnerable in the situation we found ourselves in, and under normal circumstances things would never have happened."

"Seems dishonest to me."

"Well, yes, I guess so, but… it's just giving the media what they want. When you think of all the good we could do, I think the end justifies the means."

"I don't know."

"Six months out of our lives is nothing, Laura. It could mean the difference between life and death for the people Medi-Aid treat. At least have a think about it."

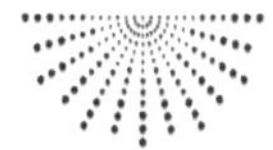

CHAPTER TEN

*L*aura gazed unseeingly out of the plane's window. Why had she agreed to Marc's ridiculous plan?

They had been in the air for hours and it was wearing a bit thin. It had started early the previous day when they had been choppered back across the island to the hospital by a team from the military base.

Marcus had arranged a brief meeting with the hospital staff, then they'd had less than an hour to pack, in order to make the cargo plane leaving after its regular run to Levati. Then on to Guam and Singapore.

To Laura, it seemed so much longer on the return trip than it had been going outbound. Now, on the final leg to Australia, Laura's hands twisted in her lap tighter and tighter. She was surprised she hadn't already passed out from breathing rapidly.

Marcus appeared calm and totally at ease. The fact that one of the flight attendants took a shine to him and flirted outrageously didn't seem to bother him one bit. It bothered her, though, more than she would care to admit. The blonde bombshell couldn't do enough for the doctor and, to Laura's mind, used any excuse to stop by his aisle seat for a chat.

Laura chided herself. What right did she have to be jealous?

He had been protective of her in the jungle, but no more than he would've been for anyone else.

This would be purely business, she knew that. His primary focus was to increase the profile of Medi-Aid, and he needed her to help.

MARCUS WAS pleased and relieved Laura had finally seen the value of the media deal. But he realised he would need to manage the publicity as best he could. It was more than likely she would pull the pin at any time if it got out of hand and she felt too overwhelmed.

He knew it was totally crazy.

He was totally crazy.

But he was determined to make it work, for both of them. The publicity for Medi-Aid was too good to pass up, even if it meant stretching the truth a little. Okay, a lot. He just hoped Laura would be able to keep up her end of the bargain.

~

LAURA'S INSIDES churned at the prospect of what lay ahead. A press conference had been organised at Brisbane airport for soon after they were due to arrive. It filled her with dread. By the time the plane started circling the airport, she was sure she would be physically ill.

Absently, she twisted the signet ring on her finger as the plane started its descent. She closed her eyes, trying to fight the waves of panic that were washing over her.

Marcus seemed not to notice her unease. As the plane taxied to the terminal, he reached a hand across to her leg and gave it a pat. Laura looked at him. His gaze was unwavering.

"It will be fine, you'll see."

She remembered the strength she had gained from that look

back when they were treating the aftermath of the drunken night's revelry. The sense of calm that rolled over her didn't last long. Someone from airport security boarded the plane and escorted them to the terminal. They were whisked through customs to a private lounge where they were met by senior airport staff and government officials, including the Minister for Foreign Affairs. It seemed a bit ludicrous that a minister of the crown was in attendance, but maybe there was political mileage to be made.

Once introductions were made, the officials got down to business.

"The press conference is scheduled in just over an hour. That should give you enough time to freshen up and catch your breath." Their luggage arrived quickly, and they were able to take advantage of the facilities to shower and change. Laura's choice of what to wear was limited. She'd travelled light. In the end, she wore a simple short-sleeved white blouse with a navy skirt and sandals, and scooped her hair into a ponytail.

She sat with a coffee, while people milled around the room talking to Marcus. He was dressed casually in tan chinos and, of course, a Medi-Aid polo shirt. She was content to remain quietly in the background.

Somebody announced it was time. Laura drained the last mouthful of her coffee and got nervously to her feet, walking over to where Marcus was getting a last-minute briefing.

"Ready?" he asked as they walked down the corridor to the room where the press conference would take place. She shook her head. "You can do this," he told her.

THEY PAUSED for a moment outside the door. The hum of the media inside was audible. As the door opened, Laura followed one of the airport representatives but was stunned by the sudden barrage of camera flashes that greeted her. She stood transfixed, for what seemed an eternity, until Marcus put a hand under her elbow and guided her to a seat behind a mountain of microphones.

Laura swallowed as the applause died down, but the cameras kept flashing. The room was far from small, but it was crammed with journalists, photographers and news cameramen all on hand to record the first words of the "Kidnap Couple", as they had been dubbed.

The Minister for Foreign Affairs read from a prepared statement, saying how pleased the government was at the release of its citizens and praising the efforts of the US military.

He handed the floor to Marcus, who gave a quick rundown of events surrounding their capture. He thanked those who had helped them, and gave a good plug for Medi-Aid at the same time.

When he indicated it was time for questions, the crowd in front of them erupted. Bewildered by the fuss, Laura watched as Marcus fielded question after question. "How were you treated?" "Were you tied up?" "What did you eat?" "How did you survive?" "What kept you going?"

On and on they went. It was hard to keep up with all the back and forth. Her head was swimming. She felt overwhelmed and on the verge of running from the room.

Laura was startled when the questions came her way. Confused for a moment, she was unable to respond until she took a deep breath and forced herself to clear her mind.

"I'm sorry if I seem a bit vague," she apologised. "When they told me there would be a press conference, I imagined a handful of reporters, not"—she gestured around the room—"this. To be honest I'm finding it more daunting than the three weeks I've just spent in captivity."

Laughter rippled around the room. She answered questions as best she could, and then came the crunch.

"When can we expect you two to be getting married?"

Laura looked at Marcus. "Um, nothing's been decided yet, we'll... um... just see how things go."

"We'd like to spend a bit of time together in the real world," Marcus put in smoothly. "Because we were together in extenuating circumstances, it will take a while to come to terms with the whole experience. But as far as I'm concerned, the sooner, the better."

Laura tried not to show her surprise.

"Show us the ring," someone shouted.

Laura obliged, lifting her left hand up, turning it for the cameras.

The press conference was quickly wrapped up. Laura followed the lead of Marcus and stood.

"Can we have a couple of shots of the two of you together?"

"Sure." Marcus stepped behind Laura as directions were shouted from all sides.

"Put your arm around her waist."

"Lean back on him."

Marcus placed his other hand lightly on her shoulder.

"Reach up and take his hand so we can see the ring."

"Look at each other."

"Smile."

"Give her a hug."

"Now a kiss."

Marcus obliged with good humour, planting a soft one on her cheek.

FINALLY WALKING out of the room was a huge relief for Laura.

"I think that went well," Marc told her.

"That's a matter of opinion."

People were still arriving in the private lounge they had returned to. Marcus took the cold drink he was offered and sat down.

"Phew, telecast live around the world. Can you believe that?"

Laura couldn't. "What was that? Did you say it was live?"

"Yep." He was relaxed about the whole thing. "Live to air and then edited for the news tonight. Amazing, isn't it?" His attention was diverted before she could respond.

~

"Ms Maxwell, your father is here." Laura turned to find her dad standing near the door.

She was shocked at how he had aged since she had last seen him, then immediately felt guilty knowing worry about her had probably been the chief cause. He looked tired and worn, more than he usually did having a young family at his age.

"Dad." She went to embrace him. He hugged her tightly.

"Babe, I'm so glad to see you again," he muttered against her hair. "You had me— us worried for a while there. Brooke sends her love. Sorry she couldn't be here, but Chloe isn't well."

Sure, she isn't. But she kept her thoughts to herself.

"The boys said to say hi. You gave us quite a scare."

"I know, Dad, I'm sorry." They caught up for a few minutes before Marcus joined them.

John Maxwell greeted the younger man. "Ah, Doctor Bradley, so you're the fellow who's managed to capture my daughter's heart."

"Yes, sir," he shook hands warmly with Laura's father, "it would appear that way."

"Well, you make sure you look after her, she means a lot to me."

"And to me. Don't worry, Mr Maxwell, I intend to do all in my power to ensure she is happy."

Fortunately, Laura wasn't taking a mouthful of water at that moment, otherwise she would have choked. She had to hand it to him, he was good. Putting an arm around her waist, he leaned down to drop a kiss on the top of her head, tucking her in against his side.

"Marc," she said, slightly embarrassed. Fake affection in front of her father. Did it get any worse than that, she wondered? She felt such a fraud. There was no hint whatsoever of anything untoward from Marcus.

She marvelled at his convincing performance.

"Sorry, I can't stay," her father was saying, "I took a late lunch to be here."

"That's okay Dad, I'll catch up with you soon." She hugged him again before he found his way out. They both turned as someone spoke to Marcus.

"Doctor Bradley, the limousine has arrived to take you and Ms Maxwell to the coast."

"Great, let's go." He slipped his arm down and caught her by the hand, but she resisted. He looked down at her.

"Would you mind telling me what this is all about?" she asked.

"All part of the deal," was all he told her as he tugged her along. Their bags hardly took up any space in the vast boot of the limousine. Laura felt horribly out of place in the luxuriously appointed car. The ride was smooth and fast and, after all the stress of the day, she became drowsy.

When Laura nodded off, Marcus slid over next to her and pulled her gently against his shoulder, wrapping an arm around her to keep her in place. Was he doing the right thing? He wasn't sure. The next few days were, by all accounts, going to be crazy. He was pretty sure if he hadn't taken her arm at the outset of the press conference, she would've turned tail and run. Not that he could have blamed her. Even he had been stunned at the media presence.

All he could do was remember he agreed to this in an effort

to raise public awareness of Medi-Aid. Laura was a reluctant participant, and he determined to do as much as possible to shoulder the bulk of the publicity load. Part of the deal he had brokered was a couple of days on the Gold Coast to catch their breath before the rounds of the media started in earnest. The limo ride was a nice bonus. Part of being buttered up by the television network and its affiliates.

~

LAURA WOKE with a start when Marcus roused her. "Come on sleepyhead, we're here." She sat up as he released her from his side. She looked out of the window, avoiding eye contact, as the car pulled up.

The chauffeur opened the door. "Ms Maxwell." He tipped his hat.

"Thank you."

"You're most welcome."

Nothing could have prepared Laura for the beauty and sheer luxury of the exclusive resort they had been taken to. She vaguely remembered reading something about the resort when it opened a couple of years back—but she never once thought she would even visit, let alone stay there.

The limousine had pulled into a covered driveway in front of the grand entrance. There was only one level, so everything blended into the lush surrounds. Marcus took her arm as he alighted from the car behind her. The wide sandstone steps were flanked either side with a matching square column about a metre high.

At the top of the stairs on each side were two huge sandstone pots with a striking orange floral arrangement in each.

The massive carved doors stood open, and her eyes widened as they walked up the half a dozen steps into the main reception area. An expanse of colour and movement surrounded her as she paused to take it all in. Elegant muted pinks were offset by marble floors and carved sandstone walls. Sofas and single chairs were scattered around the area, with a cluster to the left of the entrance and another grouping at the back of the room. A fountain provided the only background noise as they crossed the foyer to the long, curved, light timber reception desk to the right. The resort manager herself came to greet them. Middle-aged with bottle-blonde hair pulled back into a bun, she was elegantly dressed in a black skirt and a salmon-pink blouse with the resort logo embroidered on the left-hand side. She reached out perfectly manicured fingers to shake hands. For some reason, Laura felt more than a little intimidated.

"Doctor Bradley, Ms Maxwell. It's a pleasure to have you stay with us. I know you will enjoy your time here. Please make use of room service. We'll do whatever we can to help you relax after that terrible ordeal." She led them outside. "There are no cars allowed past the main reception area. Generally, our guests walk, or bike. There are complimentary bicycles available or you can take one of these golf buggies to get around." A covered six-seater buggy pulled up in front of them.

"Carl, here, will take you to your accommodation. I look forward to having you dine with me sometime while you are here."

With that, she handed each of them a room key, and waited until Carl had manhandled the luggage into the back section and set the buggy in motion. They were driven around the beautiful sub-tropical gardens to their villa. Surrounded as it was by lush, green, well-cared-for vegetation, it was very private and quiet. There was no sign of any other buildings, although they knew from the signage they were there, set back amongst the greenery. The low-set, sand-coloured building was not readily visible from the narrow roadway that ran the perimeter of the resort.

Carl pulled up, killed the engine, and walked to the back of the cart to retrieve the luggage. As they followed their driver along a curved pathway to a carved timber door, Marcus held her hand. Carl put the luggage down as he waited for Marcus to open the door and step back for Laura to enter first. Both thanked him as he set their bags down just inside the entrance.

~

ON THE LEFT as they walked in was a round, grey four-seater dining table with matching upholstered chairs with black metal frames. To the right was a lounge area with the usual television attached to the wall and the obligatory artwork—in this case a watercolour beach scene—hanging between the television and a sliding door that led to an outside garden area. A black leather three-seater lounge faced the television and a couple of single chairs angled towards the sliding door. Alongside the lounge was a sleek, compact kitchen—not that either of them planned on making use of it.

Marcus picked up her suitcase and directed her to the main bedroom once they had been left alone.

"I'm happy to use the second bedroom."

"Thanks."

He disappeared to retrieve his duffle bag and headed for the room adjacent to hers.

Obviously keen to get down to the surf, he emerged a few minutes later with a room towel over his shoulder, ready to swim. Laura wasn't inclined to swim—it wasn't hot enough for her. Still, she decided to follow Marcus through their private courtyard along a winding track that joined with ones from other villas, leading right down through the foreshore vegetation to the beach: a private stretch owned by the resort which provided its own lifeguard.

A handful of people were still on the sand at that late hour. Two or three were in the ocean. Laura wandered along the edge of the water, watching the ebb and flow of the waves as the tide crept in slowly. The sound of the surf was a soothing balm.

Finding a spot, she sat for a long time with her eyes closed, listening. The smell of the salt spray helped calm her taut nerves. She inhaled deeply, drawing the fresh ocean breeze into her body. Pulling her knees up to her chest, she dropped her head onto her crossed arms and willed herself to relax. Laura had no idea how long she sat there.

~

WHILE HE WAS in the water, Marcus had kept an eye on Laura as she wandered aimlessly along the beach, stopping to inhale the salt air. By the time he was ready to come out of the surf he saw she was curled up on the sand next to his towel. He was reluctant to disturb her peace and quiet.

Reaching for his towel, he held it away to shake off the sand, drying his face and torso quickly. He stood in front of her and waited until she finally looked up and acknowledged him. There was a flash of something in her dark eyes. Fear, maybe. But it was gone quickly.

He instantly doubted the wisdom of what he was asking of her. All he wanted to do was take her into his arms and tell her everything would be okay. But he shoved the guilt and disquiet down deep, instead holding his hand out to her.

She accepted his offer to pull her to her feet. "How was it?"

"Absolutely invigorating. I really needed that." He slung the towel around his hips and fastened the end. Running his fingers through his thick blond hair, Marcus put a hand under Laura's arm to walk back with her. "Would you like to go out for a meal?"

"No thanks, I think I'll just have something from room service and have an early night."

"Good idea, you'll want to be rested for the magazine interview tomorrow."

"Already? I was hoping it wouldn't be for a couple of weeks yet."

"Sorry to disappoint you, but they are due to go to press in a couple of days and they decided they wanted us for the cover story. Apparently, they think we will boost their circulation figures somewhat."

"Great, I can hardly wait."

~

LATER, Laura sat across from Marcus as he switched on the television to watch the news broadcasts. The press conference was the lead story on every station. He flipped from channel to channel before settling on one. Laura viewed the story with embarrassment. She thought she looked like a startled kangaroo caught in the beam of car headlights.

"They used some Medi-Aid footage, that's good," Marcus commented, looking pleased.

Laura excused herself a short time later. She tried to sleep. Since their capture, some nights had been better than others. At times, she was hardly disturbed at all. Then other nights the bad dreams haunted her every time she closed her eyes. Always the same. Running, running through the night jungle. Stumbling and falling as she tried to evade her captors. Hearing them shouting and crashing through the foliage behind her. Gaining on her. Exhausted, she fought on. She must not be caught, but they were getting closer. Despite her desperate efforts, she knew they were closing in. Suddenly she was surrounded. She couldn't breathe. She couldn't make anyone out, they were faceless monsters in the dark, but their voices… she knew! A circle of leering, groping men. They wanted her.

Laura woke up gasping for air. She sat up with the sweat rolling down, her body damp. Gradually, her breathing slowed, and she could lie down, reluctant to go to sleep in case she was chased again. Morning would be a relief.

CHAPTER ELEVEN

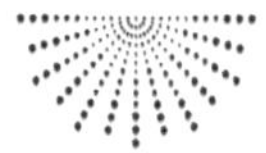

$\mathcal{E}$vidently, Marcus had already been in the surf by the time Laura struggled up the next morning. Hair still damp and dressed casually in long black shorts and a blue striped open neck shirt, he sat helping himself to a huge breakfast of cereal, fruit and fresh baked croissants.

"I ordered enough for both of us; I hope you don't mind."

She shook her head and took the chair opposite.

There was a pile of newspapers folded on the seat between them. Laura was curious but at the same time worried about what they might contain. She pretended to ignore them but, in the end, she couldn't help but pick them up.

"I got as many different papers sent around as I could... front page on all of them. Some good reports among them and most have a couple of paragraphs about Medi-Aid. I think the publicity machine is off to a good start."

He watched her reaction as she picked up the top paper. She was shocked by the size of the photo, which took up nearly the whole page. Under the headline, "They're Back", was a photo of them together after the interview. The caption read, "Levati kidnap couple Doctor Marcus Bradley and Nurse Laura Maxwell pictured at their press conference yesterday, details page three."

Laura opened the paper and her eyes widened at the next photo, of him kissing her. There was a smaller one of Marcus talking to reporters with her watching him. She saw he had hold of her hand on the tabletop. For the life of her she couldn't remember him doing that, but there it was, in black and white. She read the accompanying text, then gave the other papers a cursory glance. The stories were similar, as were the choice of photos used. She put them back in a pile on the chair.

"WELL?" he asked her. "What do you think?"

She shrugged at him. "They're okay I guess."

He narrowed his gaze at her. "What's wrong?"

She hesitated before replying to him. "I'm not sure I feel comfortable with all of the fuss."

He figured that, and he wasn't sure his next words would bring her any comfort. "It's only just the beginning, Laura."

"I know, that's what scares me the most."

"We'll get through it… together."

"I… well… I… just…"

"I know it's hard to comprehend, and I don't get the level of media interest myself, but the publicity is too good to pass up."

Laura sighed, and bit her lip to refrain from commenting. Reaching over to pick up a croissant, she stiffened as Marcus laid a hand on her arm.

"You won't do anything foolish, will you?"

"What… whatever do you mean?"

"Anything we do in the next couple of months will be news. If you tried to make a run for it, that's what will be in the papers and on the television news reports. I want you to promise that you won't take off somewhere." She didn't answer. "Laura, look at me." His voice was firm.

She glanced up, and his steady gaze was all it took to

convince her she needed to stay the course. "I… promise…" was all she could manage.

Seeming satisfied with that, he released her arm and let her finish eating before he dropped the next bombshell. "As soon as you are finished, we're going to hit the shops."

"Whatever for?"

"Some clothes for the photo shoot this afternoon."

She started to protest.

"Neither of us have anything particularly suitable," he informed her. "It's all about image now. Something we will have to carefully cultivate."

~

THAT MARCUS HAD A PARTICULAR "IMAGE" in mind was evident as he insisted on taking her to upmarket boutiques. Laura would never have considered darkening their doorways, let alone trying anything on. She gulped at some of the price tags, but Marcus never batted an eyelid.

"Marcus, I can't afford this," she told him quietly as he told the assistant they'd take the dress.

"Don't fret, it's my shout."

"No, I can't—"

He cut her off rather abruptly. "Just think of it as part of the deal."

After purchases at a couple more shops, Marcus announced it was time for the hairdresser. He took her to an exclusive salon where they seemed to be expected. Laura was ushered to a seat at once. Marcus spoke to the manager, then disappeared out the door.

"Ms Maxwell, what a pleasure to have you with us today." The manager, dressed all in black, was tall and thin with closely cropped jet-black hair and a goatee beard. He stood behind Laura and picked up her hair.

"I think we will just give your hair a good trim and reshape it slightly. You have such beautiful hair but, darling, it really needs a good protein treatment."

Once she submitted herself to Paul, she relished the process of having her hair done. She closed her eyes. It was heavenly to have someone massage her head gently. The hairdresser talked away twenty to the dozen about this and that—some of his other clients and their social lives. He questioned her at length about her ordeal. Laura tried to answer him as politely as possible, but she really didn't want to talk about herself.

She had to admit, Paul was a miracle worker. The result was amazing. Her hair had developed a wave after its cut, then Paul used a blow dryer and styling gel to give it more body and bounce. He swept her long fringe back and loaded it with spray for the photo shoot. Then the make-up artist got to work.

Marcus returned with a couple of bags in either hand just as Paul pronounced her finished. He walked over as Paul pulled the cape from her shoulders and she stood up to join him at the counter. She could tell he approved of the stylist's work.

Laura hardly ate any lunch because of the swarm of butterflies in her stomach. As for having a rest after lunch, well, forget that. She didn't want to mess up Paul's handiwork.

Later, while she dressed, she had to admit Marcus had a good eye for clothes. The short-sleeved white dress she slipped on had a rounded neckline, low but not too revealing. Cinched at the waist by a large white belt, the dress fell in layers to halfway down her calves. On her feet, strappy, white, mid-heeled sandals.

It looked and felt very feminine and, with her dark colouring, slightly exotic. She had just checked herself in the mirror for the umpteenth time when she heard Marcus walk across to answer a knock on the door of the villa.

~

MARCUS LOOKED towards Laura's bedroom, but there seemed to be little movement. It was show time. The moment before he opened the front door to admit their guests, he wondered again if he was doing the right thing.

Despite her initial reticence, he had been able to help Laura choose several outfits she would be able to wear over the next few days. He decided not to burden her with too much all at once; she was overwhelmed enough already. For now, it would be on a need-to-know basis. A bit at a time. He just had to get her through this afternoon.

~

TAKING a few deep breaths to calm herself, Laura wandered out to where the magazine people were waiting to be introduced. Marcus came forward to meet her, wearing white pants and matching shoes. Casual, with all the hallmarks of designer quality. He also wore a white t-shirt under a pale blue overshirt rolled at the sleeves to show his muscled arms. The tan had paled over their three weeks of confinement, but she knew it would soon be back in place.

He drew her over to the visitors. "Laura, I'd like you to meet reporter Kelly White from *The Australian Women's Journal*, and Sean Cullen who will be doing the photographs."

Kelly White was a petite woman about Laura's own age with short brunette hair, dressed like a successful businesswoman in a pair of black tailored trousers and a cream blouse under a black jacket. The reporter wore sky-high red heels that added a pop of colour, along with matching necklace and earrings. Laura didn't feel as put together as she had a few moments earlier.

Middle-aged Sean Cullen was grungy by comparison, in ripped jeans and a navy polo shirt. His long scruffy hair was pulled back into a ponytail. His beard, likewise, scruffy with touches of grey throughout.

AFTER WHAT LAURA had been through in the jungle, Marcus didn't like the way Sean Cullen was sizing her up. In fact, he had to stop himself from shielding her from the older man's gaze. He tried to keep telling himself the man was working out how best to photograph her, but he wasn't convinced. Then again, he would defy any man not to be checking her out in that outfit. Even though he had seen the dress when she had tried it on earlier in the day at the store, now—coupled with the hair and makeup—it almost made him forget what he was supposed to be doing.

Marcus motioned for her to sit with him on the lounge and he quickly closed the gap between them. Leaning back, he draped one arm across the top of the seat behind her. With the other he picked up her nearest hand and held it firmly.

Kelly sat opposite while Sean set up his equipment.

Marcus fervently hoped that to the two visitors they seemed like a couple in love. He could tell Laura was trying not to squirm as he leaned over and gently kissed her cheek. She turned her head slightly to look at him. His eyes captured hers and he wanted to just sit and stare into them. He shook his head slightly as Kelly started the interview and he pulled himself from Laura and turned back to the reporter.

ONCE MARCUS BEGAN TO SPEAK, the reporter seemed captivated. As Laura listened, she wondered if they had been in the same place at the same time. He was making it sound... not more adventurous or romantic even... just... well... different, but then he probably viewed the whole experience in a totally different light to her. It didn't seem quite so bad the way he related it.

Kelly turned her attention to Laura. Initially, the questions were innocuous enough. Why she went to Levati, first impressions and so on. Answering questions about their capture was a little harder, any words she chose to describe their situation and her reaction to it seemed inadequate. She glossed over the events that led to her nightmares; it was too personal to share with other people. Sooner or later, though, she knew the questions would change.

"Was there an immediate attraction between the two of you?"

MARCUS FELT Laura shift uncomfortably beside him. This was what he had been dreading.

"Well, we didn't get off to a very good start," he heard her admit. "Marcus was barely in the hospital when there was a medical emergency—a stabbing. We needed to go into surgery immediately. I'd had a bad day and didn't perform as well as I should have. The patient was fine by the way, but the good doctor wasn't impressed."

"She more than made up for it later," he interrupted, defending her. "Operating on the general's son under the conditions we were in was extremely difficult and she came through with flying colours."

"So, when did you two start to hit it off?"

Laura was hard pressed to come up with a suitable answer. She tried to get her brain into some sort of gear, but her thoughts were scattered. She had no idea how to respond.

"Um… well… I guess it was a gradual process."

"What did you think of his marriage ploy?"

"I was somewhat taken aback." She felt the slight increase of pressure on her hand and tried to choose her words carefully. "Obviously, it turned out to be a good idea. It helped deflect some unwanted attention. I'm thankful he had the presence of mind to come up with the plan."

"Can you tell us when the big day will be?"

Like never, she thought. But obviously, there was no way she could articulate that. "Look, that's a fair way down the track at the moment." Uncomfortable at the lie, she tried to force herself to make eye contact with the reporter.

"You'll be the first to know," Marcus said to Kelly.

FINALLY, it was time for the photos.

"Okay you two, I want some nice lovey-dovey shots." Sean Cullen took over. "Marc, sit back in the corner of the lounge there. Yep, that's it. Laura, just get up for a minute. Now Marc, stretch one leg out along the length of the seat and leave the other on the floor." He paused while Marcus complied with the request. "Righto, Laura sit back down, in the gap there against Marc... lean back... fine... now cuddle up a bit... arms around her... lean back a little more Laura. Great... just right... hang on... hold that." Sean was more than a little bossy, but he obviously knew what he wanted. "Laura, I want you to go around behind Marc. Just relax there a bit, mate. Here, Laura, sit on this chair," he said, pulling one from the other side of the room. "That'll make you the right height. Good, now lean forward and put your arms around his neck. No, further down. That's right. Now tip your head in a little more... woah... that's it."

The "Kidnap Couple" did as they were told, until the photographer was satisfied he had enough shots. He looked outside. "Sun's going down, we could get some great beach shots as well."

Kelly nodded and led the way down to the beach, pausing to reach down and take off her heels. Laura slipped off her own sandals, trying to ignore the handful of curious onlookers as Marcus rolled his trousers up.

"Right, just hold hands and go for a walk up the sand along the water's edge."

"I feel ridiculous," she muttered to him once they were out of earshot.

"Think of all the publicity."

"Yeah, right," she said crossly.

Marcus just pulled her in close. He wrapped his arm around her shoulder and leaned his cheek against the top of her hair. Whatever products the hairdresser had used were getting to him. He tried to take a deep breath to inhale all the sweetness without her noticing.

"Okay guys, you can come back now," Sean called to them.

The tide was on its way in and she tugged at his hand.

"Where do you think you are going?"

"Out of this water before my dress gets ruined."

"Oh, no you don't." Before he realised what he was doing he had scooped her up and walked out into the water.

"Marc, put me down!"

He refused to listen to her protests and kept walking. Pretending to trip, he feigned dropping her.

"Marc!" she squealed, and buried her face into his neck and hung on.

He just chuckled, pleased with himself for coming up with the idea. Having her arms around his neck, the warmth of her breath against his cheek and her scent was something he could get very used to. It was all he could do to stop himself leaning his head against hers and breathing deeply.

"Keep going," the photographer called.

"You beast." She thumped his chest.

He swung her down to stand in the water and turned her face to his. Pushing a strand of hair back from her face, he lightly ran a finger down her cheek. Her eyes fluttered. In the split second before his mouth reached hers, something shifted between them. Although he wasn't sure what it was, exactly. His gentle insistence won her response. She put one hand to his chest as he pulled her up against him and moulded her body into his. Her other hand slipped around his waist.

LAURA REACHED up and pulled him down closer. Her nerve endings were firing like crazy. His fingers were splayed across her back as he held her in place. She couldn't explain what was happening in that moment, but it was good. Really. Good. No, it was amazing! They could have been the only ones on the beach. The water swirled around up to her knees. The edge of her skirt clung to her legs, but she was oblivious as his kiss deepened.

Suddenly he pulled her arms down gently and set her aside slightly, keeping his hands on her waist. The cool air rushed at her, replacing the warmth from his body. She wanted to lean into him again, so she could feel his arms around her and his lips on hers.

"I hope we've been convincing enough," he whispered. His words stung as reality set in. It was all part of the act. At least it was for Marcus, but Laura wasn't sure about her own role anymore.

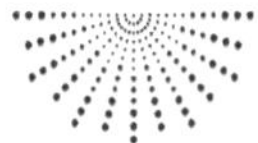

CHAPTER TWELVE

*L*aura sat up, gasping for air, pushing her fist against her chest. The bedside clock read two am.

Sleep was elusive, so eventually she wandered out to the lounge area. The rhythmic sounds of the ocean rolled in through the huge sliding doors. Tucking her feet under her, Laura curled up on the couch in the darkness and tried to empty her mind of its turmoil.

She didn't know how long she sat there. Eyes closed, she felt a movement near her as Marcus sat down alongside her.

"Can't sleep?" he asked quietly.

Laura looked in his direction and just shrugged her shoulders but could tell he wasn't going to go away any time soon. The silence stretched on, until Laura finally got up courage to speak. "It's the same thing over and over." She shifted position. "On a good night, I'm only disturbed once, but other times it replays all night long. Every time I close my eyes it comes back to haunt me… I'm running through the jungle at night and they are after me. It's awful, I can hear them crashing through the undergrowth, shouting and yelling. There's no moonlight, so I can't see where I'm going, and I stumble and trip over tree roots and branches. Every night, the sheer terror is tangible. They are getting closer and closer. Then suddenly I'm surrounded by them. They jeer and start to grope and push me around… that's usually where I wake up… I don't expect you to understand, but it's awful to keep reliving the whole experience time after time, night after night." Laura dropped her head into her hands, shuddering at the memory.

Marcus reached out to push a lock of hair back behind her ear and rested his hand on her shoulder. "Laura, you're not the only one with disturbed nights."

"What do you mean?" she faltered, fighting back tears.

"I've got my own night demons to deal with."

"You? But you seem to have come through without any problems."

"No, not quite," he told her, dropping his hand to his knee. She couldn't quite make out his features in the dark, but she could hear it in his voice easily enough. "Although I admit mine don't seem to be as… intense or as frequent as your nightmares seem to be… Same situation, different scenario." He paused before continuing, "The soldiers have dragged you off screaming and I'm trying desperately to get to you, but the direction of your screams keeps changing and I can't find a way to get to you…" He trailed off, staring off into a point in the darkness.

Laura all at once felt ashamed that she had assumed he was okay. She'd had no idea that she wasn't alone. Putting a hand on his arm, the tears now streaming down her face, she leaned towards him. "Marc, I'm so sorry… I had no idea…"

He covered her hand with his own.

"Sweetheart, you have enough problems of your own to deal with without mine as well." He patted her hand. "It's okay, Laura."

But it wasn't okay. The emotional floodgates burst open. Laura sobbed uncontrollably.

His automatic reaction was to pull her gently into his arms, up against his chest, and let her cry it all out. She clung to him as he rubbed a hand over her back to soothe her, angry with himself that he hadn't noticed how close to the edge she had been. Seeing her in so much torment was twisting his insides. Not knowing the best way to help her was agonising. So, he just sat and held her close.

Gradually, her sobs lessened, and she became quiet. Marcus eased himself back into a more comfortable position.

LAURA'S ANGUISH was finally spent. She felt her body relax against Marc, secure in his arms. She closed her eyes—just for a minute, she told herself. She noticed the warmth of his body through the thin material of his t-shirt and found comfort in the steady thud of his heartbeat in her ear. Just a little longer...

LAURA WOKE up in her own bed, vaguely aware of having been carried there sometime around daybreak. She remembered a kiss on the forehead and some soothing words. Then sleep, free of nightmares, for a few hours.

Silence greeted her in the villa. A message from Marc indicated he would be away for most of the day, working on a possible interview schedule, and told her not to expect to see him around.

In fact, he wasn't there much at all over the next few days. It felt strange in a way; she was so used to having him around—even if it had been forced companionship—that she kept looking for him. She felt a bit lost. She spent her days swimming and lying around, enjoying the wonderful food but studiously avoiding the papers and television.

The nightmares had reduced in intensity and she fervently wished they would just go away completely. If she found she couldn't get back to sleep, she would get up for a while. Marcus would inevitably join her, not saying anything in particular—him just being there was a huge comfort.

She never gave way to tears again, so he never had cause to hold her.

ON THEIR LAST NIGHT, Marcus decided to take her to the resort restaurant where they enjoyed a meal. She was quiet, and he had to work hard to draw her into any sort of conversation. He missed the animated discussions they'd had in the confined quarters of their prison hut.

Her fragility concerned him and he was worried how she would cope with what lay ahead, but he had to push on. The publicity for Medi-Aid was so important. He had to take the opportunities while they were available and hope that the consequences weren't too traumatic for either of them.

"Tomorrow, we're driving to Brisbane. We have radio interviews most of the morning and after lunch we are going to Mt Coot-tha to pre-record an interview for *Australia Tonight*."

He watched her reaction carefully. She hesitated and nodded slowly. He told her about the interviews and the sort of questions they might be asked, and suggested possible responses. Laura seemed worried about the whole process.

He was more than a little concerned himself. He had no idea if she would be able to survive the media scrutiny that persisted while they were flavour of the month.

He wasn't sure he would, for that matter.

CASUALLY DRESSED in jeans and Medi-Aid polo shirts, Marcus and Laura drove up to Brisbane to do the rounds of the radio stations. After the first nerve-wracking interview, Laura found the process a little easier, especially as similar questions were asked everywhere they went.

"Would you like something to eat?" he asked when they finally finished

"If you don't mind, could we get something on the run? I'd love to get home for a while seeing as we've got a bit of time to kill."

"Here you go, then." He tossed her the car keys. "You can drive."

She felt small behind the wheel as she struggled to familiarise herself with the hire car, and she felt a bit rusty after so many weeks away. Once they were out of the city, traffic on the South East Freeway flowed well. She relaxed, feeling more at ease behind the wheel. The sign for her exit loomed and she took the off-ramp.

"What'll it be?" she asked. "Red Rooster, KFC, McDonalds or Hungry Jacks?"

"Maccas will be fine, although I must admit I prefer an upmarket restaurant to fast food." Placing an order at the drive-through window, they picked up their meal and Laura continued to her apartment.

MARCUS WAS curious to see where Laura lived—to see her on her home turf. The apartment was in a quiet, leafy street close to local shops. After pulling into the visitor's parking bay in front of the cream-brick three-storey building, Laura rummaged through her gear to find her keys. He hauled out her suitcase while she grabbed her cabin bag and led the way up to the top level, dropping her bag inside the door as she raced around opening windows and the sliding door onto the tiny balcony. Marcus set the takeaway packets on the small round four-seater kitchen table.

"The plates are in the second cupboard to the right of the refrigerator," she called over her shoulder as she disappeared into her bedroom with her luggage. "I'm just going to dump this lot. Won't be a minute."

Marcus looked around her apartment. It was small and comfortable, homey even. She wasn't given to fancy homewares. Everything was neat and organised. There were few personal items on display. Souvenirs from earlier travels on a small set of display shelves to one side of the television cabinet. On the other side, a matching bookcase. A handful of photos dotted the living area, but not much else. He knew more about her from their talks in the hut in Levati than he would've been able to glean from studying her apartment.

OVER LUNCH, they talked about the morning's radio interviews. Marcus seemed pleased enough with how they had gone and gave Laura a few suggestions he thought might come in handy for the upcoming television interview.

She told Marcus to make himself at home. "If we are going to be on the road for a while, I guess I'll have to change my wardrobe and repack."

She went to her room and upended her bags, sorting her clothes to be washed and sliding the door of her wardrobe open.

"Don't tell me you want to approve my clothing choices?" she asked as Marcus joined her.

"In a word, yes."

"You're kidding, right?" She looked at him as he shook his head. "You're not kidding? Don't you think you're overdoing things a little?"

"For the next few months you and I are engaged, so you'll have to dress for the part of the fiancée of a high-profile surgeon."

She opened her mouth to argue the point, but thought better of it and sat on her bed. "Go for it."

The sight of Marcus going carefully through her clothes was unnerving.

After a few minutes, he shook his head. "Looks like you will be going shopping in the next few days."

"No way. I'll just make do with what I have." She bristled.

"It's part of your job as a Medi-Aid ambassador."

"I didn't ask for the job," she retorted, getting up.

"Nobody forced you into the position."

"I would've been made to feel selfish and uncharitable if I hadn't."

"Your conscience is not my problem."

"Don't you dare!" she accused him. "You played it to the hilt, and you know it—so I would agree to help the poor and marginalised that your organisation support."

"And it's such a noble thing you are doing too, Laura," he taunted.

"Why. You. Swine." She drew the words out as she stood toe to toe with him. Her hand twitched. She really wanted to slap him. But it was like he read her mind. In the next breath, he bent and kissed her fiercely. Before she had a chance to react, he let her go suddenly.

"You've agreed to take on the job, Laura"—he struggled to catch his breath—"and as the public face of Medi-Aid, like it or not, there are dress standards and behaviour requirements, as there are in any job description."

She took in the set of his jaw and the glint in the blue eyes. "Damn you, Marcus Bradley," she flung at him, and wheeled out of the room. She sat in one of the lounge chairs and fumed, unable to fathom why sometimes Marcus made her so angry.

Maybe it was some sort of defensive mechanism when he got too close. She had no idea.

~

WHAT HAD POSSESSED HIM? He had no idea why he'd reacted the way he did, and now here he was sorting through her clothes, for goodness' sake. At least it gave him a few minutes to calm down. Why did this matter so much? Picturing her in the clothes as he rifled through her wardrobe helped the decision-making process. Med-Aid. It was all about the Medi-Aid image and hers… well…

She was still sitting there in the lounge when he emerged a few minutes later.

"I'm sorry to be such an embarrassment to you," she said.

Stopping mid-way across the room, he sighed. "You know the old saying: clothes maketh the man? Well, you are a beautiful woman and you should dress accordingly. All eyes should be drawn to you every time we walk into a room."

She looked up at him and caught his eyes for what seemed a long time—that snap of awareness he'd noticed on the beach. She dropped her head, breaking the connection. Irresistibly drawn to her, he barely stopped himself from going over to where she sat.

"I've pulled out some clothes that will be suitable. The burgundy dress we bought down the coast will be good for the interview tonight." When she didn't reply, he went on, "I'll be back to pick you up in ninety minutes."

Enough time to backtrack to his inner-city hotel to shower and change. At least that was the plan. He checked in, but got distracted once in his room. The balcony view over the Brisbane River pulled him in. He sat immersed in the scene for half an hour or more, trying to calm his thoughts. Laura was having a stronger and stronger effect on him. While they were in the jungle, he had successfully pushed any developing feelings aside. Getting through each day had been hard enough without adding extra emotion into the mix.

Now? He wasn't sure how he would be able to get through this. He didn't want to pretend to be the doting fiancé only for it all to end somewhere down the track. But what to do about it was another matter.

IT MUST HAVE BEEN a good thirty minutes before Laura moved from her chair. The way Marcus had looked at her when he said she was beautiful had sent a delightful shiver through her body. He wanted everyone to look at her when they were together. How would she ever be able to live up to that? Then she'd had to force herself to look away from his eyes, in case she melted on the spot.

Laura was ready, if reluctant, in the burgundy dress. The length had been way shorter than she was comfortable with when she'd tried it on, and she was sure it was even shorter now even though she knew that wasn't possible. It did show off her legs. *When did they get so long?* she wondered.

Marcus arrived wearing a burgundy shirt, tie-less, with the top two buttons left undone, with a charcoal jacket and matching trousers. She had to hand it to him, he had a wonderful sense of style. It was no wonder he expected her to be the same. But she had no idea how she could ever achieve that. She was surprised he wasn't wearing blue; it was obviously his favourite colour and the shade he wore changed the intensity of his eyes.

THE CAR TRIP up Mt Coot-tha, where the television stations were based, was uncomfortably quiet. Neither of them spoke much. Laura was trying not to have a meltdown over the whole upcoming "being on camera" thing. She couldn't see why Marcus wasn't able to handle it on his own. Print media was one thing, but television? Okay, it wasn't live, but it was the highest rated current affairs program in the country with several awards to its name—including for the host, Mike Martin.

They were directed straight into makeup and then led onto the set for the interview. A young woman in jeans and a t-shirt wearing a headset fussed around, miking them up and attaching an earpiece to each of them. Once it was in place, Laura was able to hear the presenter in the Sydney studio. Wiping her hands repeatedly on the edge of her dress, she tried to ignore the camera and the rest of the people involved in the studio cross. No matter how many times she closed her eyes and took a supposedly-calming breath, she was still overwhelmed.

Marcus reached over and took her hand. His calm demeanour helped settle her nerves.

Mike Martin chatted with them both for a few minutes to help put them at ease, before launching into the interview itself. Many of the questions were the same ones they had already answered.

But there were others.

"So, Laura, what was the first thing you did after you arrived at the military base?"

"Ate the first decent meal in over three weeks."

"Which was?"

"I don't rightly remember, it was just food, but delicious down to the last mouthful."

"I believe you nearly used up the base's water supply in the shower."

"So they tell me. After going without a shower for so long, it was wonderful to be able to enjoy one again. I love my showers and I guess they'll play a significant role in coming to terms with everything."

"How do you think you are coping?"

"Some days are better than others," she admitted, casting a glance at Marcus for support, unsure how much she needed to reveal, and not really wanting to say anything. Much of that was still raw and pushed down as far as possible. Marcus squeezed her hand. "The nightmares are hardest to come to grips with."

"Can you tell us some more about your nightmares?" She looked at Marcus, who nodded slightly.

"They resulted from an incident that happened one night, Mike, that's all I'm prepared to say."

"Marcus?"

"Some of the soldiers got drunk one night, Mike, and caused some trouble. I think that's all that needs to be said."

"Were you mistreated in any way?"

"No, not physically," Marcus continued, "but the mental strain was hard at times."

"I believe you got to know some of the guards, Marcus?"

"Somewhat. We soon got to know which ones were a little friendlier. A couple would let us out of the hut if we kept to a defined area. We looked forward to getting out, even if just for a short while."

"So, what exactly had happened to the general's son?"

"He'd been seriously wounded—shot—in a skirmish of some sort."

"And then what happened?"

"We were called in to treat him and it quickly became evident that surgery was required."

"I don't imagine for one minute that you had anything much available to work with. Few instruments if any, no way of sterilising, no gowns…"

"Just what we grabbed from the Land Rover after they spiked the tyre and demanded we go with them. We just had to do the best we could with what we had."

"I take it he lived?"

"Yes. It was pretty touch-and-go all the way."

"Amazing stuff. And was that the bargaining chip you used to try and gain your freedom?"

"It didn't seem to make any impression on the general," Laura told Mike. "Then a few days later, early in the morning, we were woken up and put into a vehicle."

"I understand you were blindfolded… then what?"

"We had no idea what was going on at first."

"Weren't you worried that they may have been going to shoot you or something?"

"No, actually. For some reason, I just felt quite okay about the whole deal."

"And you got dumped on the side of a jungle track, I believe. So tell us what happened then."

"We were on our own. Marcus seemed to recognise the area and eventually we stumbled into the perimeter of the US military base. We followed the fence line until we got to a check point."

"I bet the guard was surprised to see you walk out of the jungle. What was his reaction?"

"Stunned. He told us how they had been helping search for us."

"Then what?"

"We were taken to the main part of the base and given food and a check-up from the doctor. We spent a few days there before coming back."

"When did you realise there was such a big reaction to your story?"

"Well, Mike," Marcus said, "the base had been getting a lot of calls from media around the world, so we knew there was a level of interest, but nothing quite prepared us for walking into that press conference."

"So, what's next for the two of you?"

"We'd like to do some promotional work for Medi-Aid. As you know, Mike, any proceeds from paid stories in the media will go straight to the Medi-Aid organisation."

The interview went on. Laura was surprised. It had been well over thirty minutes since they got underway, although she knew it would be edited to probably ten minutes at the most. And then Mike dropped the questions she hated.

"What about your future plans? Has there been any talk of a wedding, and maybe starting a family?"

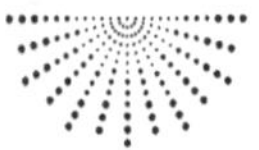

CHAPTER THIRTEEN

Once out of the studio, Marcus drove a little further along Sir Samuel Griffith Drive. They stopped at the mountain café to grab a quiet cuppa and admire the panoramic views over the entire city of Brisbane and out to Moreton Bay.

Under a scattering of white clouds on a blue backdrop, the grey-blue of the city buildings near the horizon blended into greenery in the foreground. Closer to the mountain, houses were evident, scattered through the foliage. The winding road to the top cut a swathe through trees lining the side of Mt Coot-tha.

Laura leaned against the lookout rail. "Where to now?"

"I thought you might like a chance to catch up with your father, so I've arranged for us to go to his place for dinner."

Laura seemed less than impressed. "You might have asked me first."

"Oh?"

"Don't I get any say in what goes on?" She walked away from him.

"Sorry, it didn't occur to me there would be an issue." He caught up to her. "I thought you'd be pleased to see your family."

She dropped into the car seat beside him, obviously

annoyed. "You probably don't remember me telling you, but my stepmother is not my favourite person in the world... and, well... taking you there is going to cause... a bit of trouble..." She trailed off, looking anywhere but at him.

"And why is that?"

"Because you're a male and you're with me. Look, I didn't tell you, but one of the reasons I moved out was because she'd hit on any guy I ever took near the place. It got a bit much after a while."

"What makes you so sure she will try it with me?" he asked, starting the car and putting it into gear.

She arched an eyebrow at him.

"Did you not hear what I just said? You're male, and you're supposed to be engaged to me."

"I think I'll be able to cope, but thanks for the heads up."

It was a slow run out to the southern suburbs. Calling it an expressway was a bit of a joke in peak-hour traffic. The car crawled along until they finally reached the required freeway off-ramp. The silence in the cabin had become unbearable. He had resorted to flicking on a drive-time radio show. Laura reluctantly gave Marcus directions to her father's house, a large four-bedroom brick and tile home in a new housing estate at Logan.

"Brooke insisted they build a new home after they got married. She refused to live in the old house for any longer than necessary—too many reminders of my mother. Mum's life has been reduced to a couple of tin trunks in the garage. I'm the only reminder of Dad's previous marriage, and even then she likes to pretend I'm her stepsister."

THERE WAS A TENSION IN HER—DIFFERENT to what he'd noticed earlier in the day. He wracked his brain to try and come up with something to distract her. He pulled into the driveway just as the streetlights came on, and hurried around to open her door. Tilting his chin, he motioned towards the house. "Do you think they would have seen us arrive?"

"I'm pretty sure I caught a glimpse of my stepmother at the window. She's a bit of a Nosey Parker."

"Good, come here a minute." Taking a chance, he took a step forward and pinned her to the side of the car with a scorching kiss. Her handbag fell to the ground as her hands grabbed at his shirt as if to steady herself.

"Cut that out!" she hissed at him.

Good, he'd thrown her off-balance. Mind you, it hadn't done much for his equilibrium either.

"Now, now, this is strictly for show. After all, we have to make sure they are convinced about our relationship. I know you can do better," he murmured, bending his head towards her again. As his lips slanted over hers, he wondered if he could pretend she wasn't being convincing enough so he could kiss her again and again.

HER DESIRE TO kick him in the shins lasted less than a millisecond. She tightened her hold on his shirt as her knees threatened to buckle under her. She closed her eyes, and the intoxicating scent of his aftershave made her head swim. Just as well he'd backed her up against the car to keep her steady or she would be in a heap on the driveway.

When he raised his head, she could only manage a weak smile, wanting to pull him back in for more.

"Much better." Retrieving her handbag from the driveway for her, he put a hand under her elbow, and guided her up to the front door.

Laura wondered if she looked as thoroughly kissed as she felt. It was hard to remember what she was supposed to be doing. Her brain was fighting to make any sort of connection, sent into meltdown by the good doctor at her side. The kiss obviously hadn't had the same effect on him. He seemed totally calm and in control.

When she hesitated to ring the doorbell, he reached out with his free hand and pushed the button, while slipping his other arm around her waist and pulling her in against his side.

The echo of the bell hadn't even died away when the door opened. Her stepmother stood there in a skimpy, low-cut red dress, her bottled-blonde hair pinned up, the makeup trowelled on. Laura thought she looked so tawdry.

"Laura, how good to see you." She leaned forward and kissed the air somewhere in the vicinity of Laura's cheek. "And you must be Doctor Bradley," she simpered.

"Pleased to meet you, Mrs Maxwell."

"Oh, but you must call me Brooke," she told him. "Come on in."

She led them through into the toy-strewn living area and cleared a space on the caramel-coloured lounge for them to sit. Tossing an armful of toys into the corner, she plopped down in a nearby armchair.

"So, Marcus, do you mind if I call you that?"

"Not at all."

"Tell me about your time in—where was it again?"

"Levati. You've probably seen the media reports."

"Yes, but I want to know more."

Laura groaned inwardly as her stepmother leaned forward, giving Marcus an eyeful of ample cleavage. Classic Brooke, not wearing anything underneath. Heaven help Marcus if she was going commando as well.

He answered all of Brooke's questions. She was captivated by Laura's fiancé and flirted outrageously with him. As was par for the course, Laura was ignored. She was sickened by the vintage display by her stepmother and it brought back bitter memories.

Her father wandered in with her baby stepsister, Chloe, and handed her to Brooke. "I think she needs her pants changed."

Brooke looked up at him in disgust. "Can't you do it?"

"No, I've come to say hello to Laura." He walked over to where she was sitting. "I'm glad you could come," he told Laura as she stood up to greet him. John Maxwell kissed his firstborn and hugged her, as Brooke flounced off with the baby. Marcus stood up beside her.

"Good to see you again, my boy," he told Marcus. "How did the interview go?"

"I was happy with it—weren't you, Laura?" She nodded her response. "I guess we will see how it turns out at seven."

"It's almost that now," her father replied, looking at his watch. He picked up a remote control and then another, and looked from one to the other. Aimed each of them in turn at the television screen. "Be blowed if I can remember which is which."

He turned to the doorway. "Keith! Jeffrey!" he called. No response. "Boys!"

Laura cast an apologetic glance in Marc's direction.

"They can't hear a damn thing when they are playing those blasted video games. 'Scuse me a minute."

Laura shook her head in despair as her father strode out of the room.

"Hey, don't look so worried," Marcus told her, hand on the back of her neck, leaning down to nuzzle against her cheek, only to pull away reluctantly when her father frog-marched his sons into the room.

"Say hello to your sister."

There was a mumbled hello from each. Keith turned the television on and flicked to the right channel.

"Brooke," her father called out, "the interview's on, come and have a look."

Mike Martin was just introducing the story. Keith and Jeffrey sat close to the big screen. Their father growled at them to move back, which they did, complaining all the while.

"Be quiet, you two," Brooke admonished them, coming into the room, snapping off the light and plonking the baby down on her father's lap before taking a chair nearby.

Laura was surprised the whole program had been turned over to their interview. In the end, not much was edited. It seemed to go okay, but she found it hard to concentrate. Marcus was having an unsettling effect on her. His arm was bent along the back of the lounge so his thumb could brush her neck. She tried to discourage him, but he wouldn't take the hint. He wrapped a loose tendril of her dark hair around his finger, caressed her cheek and ran his fingers through her thick hair. Reaching up, she grabbed his hand, but then his other arm moved across and the whole process started over, only halted when the living room lights were switched on again. The lazy grin he shot her warmed her cheeks. He seemed to be enjoying the role of doting fiancé.

They sat around discussing the interview until dinner was announced. It was the usual three-ring circus. The noise level was high as everyone talked at once. The two boys were being bad mannered and obnoxious, and for the most part her father ignored them. Chloe screamed in her highchair, refusing to eat the meal that was served to her.

Laura was mortified by her family's behaviour, and wished the ground would open and swallow her. As soon as she was reasonably able, Laura made an excuse for them to leave. She would've run down the path, only Marcus was in no hurry, insisting on draping his arm around her waist. Reaching the hire car, he continued to hold her while he reached into the pocket of his jacket for the key.

"Okay, I think you've gone over the top. You can drop the act now."

He said nothing as he helped her into the car. She made a big pretext of rummaging through her bag looking for her apartment keys, as he got in beside her. Pulling the bunch of keys out at last, she tossed them into her lap and dropped her bag onto the floor near her feet. Leaning back, she closed her eyes wearily, hoping Marcus would realise she didn't want to talk. He obliged for a few minutes.

"Your father seems a nice enough fellow."

"He's changed a lot since he remarried."

"In what way?"

"My father was a strict disciplinarian. The house was very ordered, our lives were ordered, everything was neat, and in its place. Now…" She shook her head. "Now it's hard to believe it's the same bloke. The kids get away with murder and the house always looks like a bomb has hit it, and he never seems to notice or mind in the slightest."

"Is he a better father this time around?"

"I don't know… I think he's gone from one extreme to the other. There's got to be a balance in there somewhere. I can't understand what someone like Brooke sees in him."

"Maybe she needs a father-type figure. She certainly doesn't seem to be the sort of woman your father would marry."

"I can't understand why he puts up with her flirting and nonsense. You can't tell me he doesn't notice all that goes on. Maybe he just chooses to ignore it."

"He might love her enough to overlook those sorts of things. Love does strange things."

"Yeah well, I'm sorry, Marcus."

"What for?"

"The whole evening. Now you know why I was less than keen when you told me we were going there. Well, it's over and done with now." She sighed heavily and closed her eyes again.

Thankfully, he didn't continue the conversation. After pulling up outside her apartment block, he was around to her door before she thought to get out. They were halfway to her apartment when she remembered she had left her bag behind in the car.

"Bother, I have to go back."

"I'll go," he offered.

"No, here." She gave him the apartment keys. "You go on ahead and open up, I'll only be a minute." Well, maybe longer— she needed a few minutes to get herself back on an even keel.

She flew back down to the rental. Collecting her handbag, she walked back up at a more sedate pace, surprised to meet Marcus on the landing.

"You didn't have to wait," she told him. "I could do with a coffee—you can come in and join me if you want…" She trailed off as he took hold of her shoulders firmly. "It's just coffee…" She looked up at him, puzzled at the seriousness of his face.

"Laura," he told her calmly, "there's been a break-in."

"A what?" she asked in disbelief.

"Someone has broken into your place… It's been trashed."

"Oh no!" she cried in anguish. Pushing past him, she stopped just inside the door, frozen, her hand clamped over her mouth.

She couldn't believe the devastation that confronted her. Furniture was upended and her possessions thrown around. The wall display unit had been pushed over and the glass doors and shelves smashed. The lounge chairs had been slashed and ripped apart.

Laura picked her way around the mess. The kitchen was worse. The pantry had been raided and almost every packet opened and thrown around the room. Flour, sugar, bread-crumbs, instant coffee, tomato sauce and other condiments were painted all over the walls. Just as well she hadn't restocked the refrigerator, otherwise the mess would've been much worse.

She was so lost in her own turmoil that she hardly heard Marcus tell her he'd rung the police. It took him several attempts to get through to her that there was no one available to come. It would probably be morning before they could send officers around.

Laura walked around in a daze, from room to room and back again. It was strange the bedroom seemed to have escaped damage. Marcus felt sure the culprit or culprits had been disturbed.

Eventually, after much persuasion, Marcus convinced Laura to turn in for the night, after assuring her he would keep watch in case the vandals returned to finish the job. The door had been kicked in and he managed to shut it, hopefully without obliterating any fingerprints. He dragged the lounge over across the door. Anyone returning would have to get past him first.

It wasn't the most comfortable of nights for either of them. He jumped at noises from outside, and dozed fitfully on and off.

The nightmare woke her up, and he found himself on the side of her bed holding her until she settled. He debated whether he should stay with her, but the possibility of the vandals coming back to finish the job returned him to his post. However, he couldn't help checking on her several times. She wasn't sleeping peacefully, but neither was he.

As he had so many other nights, he blamed himself for insisting she accompany him on the clinic run that day.

Around seven in the morning he snagged a clean towel and snuck into the bathroom for a shower to help him face the day. A quick rummage through the vanity turned up a razor, albeit one with a pink handle. Her shampoo smelled good on her, but he took a pass on using it for himself. Finding a stash of travel lotions, he took a miniature shampoo bottle into the shower.

He left his shirt off in favour of the black tee he had worn underneath it. He would have preferred to kick off his shoes as well, but with all the broken glass around it wasn't an option. In the mess of the kitchen he was amazed to find a small amount of coffee still in the bottom of the jar that lay on the floor by the oven, enough for a couple of weak drinks.

Now to find coffee mugs. Broken crockery was all over the place. It looked like the intruders had tossed stuff over the kitchen bench to smash wherever it landed. How the neighbours hadn't heard anything was baffling. Ah, there was a travel mug in the far corner of the lounge. He also found a takeaway cup on its lonesome in a cupboard where the rest of the mugs and drinking glasses would have sat.

He found the kettle, hoping it would still boil water. Success.

Laura eventually emerged, looking worse for wear in faded grey track pants, a pink singlet top that was a little too revealing, and a pair of canvas slip-ons. He handed her a coffee and righted a dining room chair for her to sit on.

Leaning on the table, he regarded her as she sat, head down, hands wrapped around the travel mug. His thoughts went in several different directions at once. She looked so vulnerable, so defeated. Dropping to his haunches in front of her, he put a comforting hand on her knee. Eventually she looked at him, fighting back tears.

"Hey, it will be alright. You'll get... we'll get through this. Go have a shower before the police get here, you'll feel better... more able to cope."

He took the empty mug out of her fingers after she drained it, put an arm under her elbow to encourage her to stand, and pointed her in the direction of the bathroom.

Ah, a shower. It always helped her to feel better about the world. But her world was spinning off its axis and she wasn't sure how to right it again. A shower would only go so far.

As much as she hated to admit it, she was grateful that Marcus had been with her when she returned home last night. His calm presence helped to ease her stress levels. Overwhelmed by the mess and destruction, she would have totally lost the plot if she'd had to face it on her own.

CHAPTER FOURTEEN

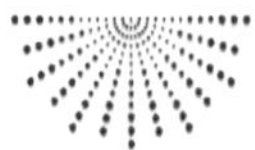

When Laura handed her list of stolen goods to the police, she hoped she had remembered everything that had been taken. The police seemed to think the break in was opportunistic, and not related to the television interview. They held little hope she would get her things back, unless the culprits were caught. On the strength of it, that didn't seem likely.

With her stereo, television and other small appliances missing, she felt violated and angry. It wasn't so much the stuff they'd taken—that was replaceable. It was that someone unknown had invaded her home, her security and peace of mind. Her home was no longer her haven—she didn't think she could ever feel safe here again. After her experience on Levati, that's what she needed above all else—a feeling of safety.

Once the police had finished taking their statements, it was a matter of waiting for the fingerprint experts before the clean-up could begin. Laura was despondent at not being able to do anything about the mess. She wandered over to the glass sliding door onto the balcony, and stood gazing out at the skyline. Her attention was caught by a vehicle pulling up on the road. Even from this distance, she could tell from the signwriting it was from Mike Martin's current affairs program. The passenger got out and spoke to the police officers who were returning to their squad car. Sudden anger overtook her as she realised what was going on.

Laura turned on Marcus. "How dare you!" she accused. "How could you do this to me?"

"Do what?" he asked.

"Of all the low-down things to do. It's bad enough I have to be on public show, but this is despicable. Why can't I just have some time to come to terms with this without sharing it with the whole country? Why can't I have some private life?"

"What are you talking about?"

She was too angry to notice he was genuinely confused. "The television crew that just pulled up outside. More precious publicity, no doubt!"

"I didn't contact them," he told her calmly.

"Liar!" She launched herself at him in fury, determined to cause him a small measure of the pain she was feeling. He merely sidestepped her, grabbing her from behind and putting his arms around her body, pinning her arms against her sides. She fought and kicked at him to no avail. He simply lifted her off the ground, holding her easily as if she were a young child throwing a temper tantrum. Her initial burst of anger spent, she slumped against him, defeated. Cautiously, he set her back on her feet but kept hold of her.

"I know you won't believe anything I say, but I had nothing to do with contacting the television station. Someone must've tipped them off."

"You're right, I don't believe you," she hissed.

The doorbell rang. They both snapped their heads in the direction of the door.

"Well, it's up to you how this story plays out. They'll be determined to do a piece no matter what you tell them. You can calm down and give them a dignified response, or you can do the wild woman thing. I know which one they'd prefer for ratings." Marcus raised his arms cautiously to release her. Fuming at him, she disappeared into the bedroom while Marcus answered the still-ringing doorbell.

She pulled clothes out of her cupboard, not really taking anything in. Jeans? She was wearing a pair. A top of some sort? She hauled off the singlet top she had put on after her shower, and stood numbly in front of her wardrobe. Which one? She discarded several choices before pulling on a white t-shirt and throwing on a lemon overshirt, leaving it unbuttoned and rolling up the sleeves. The canvas pull-on shoes would have to do.

Laura stood in front of the mirror, her head in turmoil, with no idea how she was even going to do any of this. Her hand was shaking visibly from anger and frustration as she brushed her hair. She pulled her hair back into a ponytail and sank onto her bed, listening to the muffled voices in the front room.

Taking more than a few deep breaths, she tried to compose herself, then grimly walked out to meet the television crew. After a few perfunctory remarks, Laura was asked to look over the damage. She was teetering on the emotional edge, just wanting to run away as far as she could. Steeling herself, she surveyed the apartment as she was asked, then got down on her haunches to sift through the broken remnants of her life.

Suddenly, her chest tightened and she found it hard to breathe. She couldn't do this anymore.

She stood up too quickly. A wave of dizziness hit and she swayed a little. Marcus was right behind her and put a comforting hand on her shoulder. Feeling the prick of tears behind her eyes, she was damned if she would give the cameraman the satisfaction of crying on national television. Turning away from the camera, she burrowed into Marc's shirt. He immediately enfolded her in his arms, and she refused to move until the reporter finally announced they had enough footage.

Marcus held her at arms' length. "Are you okay?"

She nodded slowly, confused by the depth of tenderness she saw in his eyes. Tears threatened again, and she walked quickly to the kitchen to gain some space by looking to fix herself a drink.

~

MARCUS INSISTED on arguing the point. "You won't be here much in the next few months. Put your gear in storage and find a new place when this is finished."

There was a flash of defiance from her. "I can't just up and leave. I still have three months left on my lease—"

"Not a problem, I'll pay it out for you."

"I can't let you do that."

"Why don't you just think of it as—"

"I know, I know, part of the deal."

He sat next to her on the floor of the lounge area, wearing heavy gloves so they could easily pick up the broken glass and other shattered bits and pieces. Knocking back his offer of getting someone in to deal with the mess, she had insisted on doing as much as possible herself.

He knew she thought it necessary for closure, to help her sort through everything, but he wasn't happy about it. There was still anger towards him simmering below the surface, but in the end she had reluctantly agreed to his proposition.

Once the news story had gone to air, Laura had been flooded with calls of sympathy from friends, and people she barely knew. He told her it would be easier to leave the answering machine to take the calls. She relented. He took it upon himself to deal with the messages and she didn't argue with him.

Of course, the newspaper wanted a story as well, so the following day another headlining feature made it to the front page. A steady stream of visitors arrived. Marcus wondered if they were genuine in their concern or just keen to have a gawk at the apartment.

In a few days, the apartment was cleared out and cleaned up. The carpet would have to be replaced. There was just no way anyone would be able to get all the splinters of glass out of the pile. Laura couldn't bring herself to sleep in the apartment any longer, and joined Marcus back at the hotel every night. They had adjoining rooms. She was grateful for his help and support, and her anger over the television interview diminished.

She left her apartment on the last day without a twinge of regret. Not at all sorry to be leaving.

CHAPTER FIFTEEN

*L*aura pushed her appointment diary back from the table and sighed. The next couple of months were going to be busy as they criss-crossed the country for various speaking engagements and other fundraising events. There was hardly a day to spare, although Marcus had scheduled a break in Cairns in a few weeks' time, presumably for Laura to meet his family.

Of course, Marcus took to the whole experience like the proverbial duck to water. For Laura, it was a slow and gradual process before she felt comfortable with the idea of speaking in front of a large gathering of people. Thankfully, Marcus did most of the talking, but she was expected to say a few words. After a while, she began to gain confidence in her ability to share something she felt people would want to hear. At first, she used carefully prepared notes, agonising over every word, with input from Marcus. Eventually, she got to the point where she could relax and speak off the cuff—not as eloquently as Marcus, but still it was an improvement.

Laura found she quite enjoyed the high school visitations that were part of their speaking engagements. It was a chance to be more casual, and the teenagers weren't backward in coming forward. She appreciated their honesty and candour. After a while, no question they threw at her could make her blush. She developed some snappy one-liners to respond to their more awkward questions.

She was buoyed by the support and encouragement she received from Marcus. Like a parent watching a child take their first tentative steps, he seemed proud of her achievements as she developed her own speaking style. She often caught him looking at her with an unfathomable expression in his eyes. He behaved impeccably, displaying enough affection in public to make it seem they were happily engaged, but otherwise she was just like a kid sister—or so it seemed to Laura. It relieved some of the tension she usually felt around him.

Her dress style also evolved. Marcus obviously approved, as he no longer felt the need to accompany her on her shopping expeditions. A good range of mix-and-match outfits served her well, with some more glamorous outfits for evening wear. If the occasion demanded, she was able to borrow clothes from some of the country's top designers. The two of them were often pictured in the social pages of newspapers in the towns and cities they visited. Laura was getting used to seeing the news reports, though she didn't like it any better.

She recalled the day early in their speaking tour when Marcus had tossed *The Australian Women's Journal* down in front of her, with Sean Cullen's photo of them on the cover. Curious, she had flipped open the cover and scanned the contents. Including photographs, the story ran to six pages. She had started to read... *They seem like any young couple in love. Handsome, successful surgeon, Doctor Marcus Bradley, is clearly besotted with the beautiful young nurse he is to marry, but the haunted look in Laura Maxwell's eyes is testament to the horror of recent events that engulfed them both...*

She had thrown the magazine down in disgust. If only they knew the truth.

MARCUS WAS in awe of the gradual transformation happening before his eyes. The confident woman who now accompanied him was a far cry from the nervous speaker she had been at first. Laura looked and sounded polished. He had to admit, she was a wonderful ambassador for Medi-Aid. Every photo of her that appeared in the social pages or the fashion columns was more precious publicity for his beloved organisation.

Keeping her at arms' length was becoming increasingly difficult. It was doing his head in to show restrained affection in public and keep her at a distance at all other times. He was struggling to think of her as a colleague when he was wanting something on a deeper level. At times, he'd catch a glimpse of something in the depths of her "melt me" brown eyes, and he would have to fight himself not to pull her into his arms and kiss her there and then. The little tastes he'd had were nowhere near enough to satisfy him.

He cursed himself for getting in this position, but it was keeping her in his life for the time being. He was grateful for every day he got to spend with her, dreading the moment when it would come to its inevitable end.

Cairns was humid and steamy. The airport taxi drove them out of town, north, to where Marcus lived.

As Laura had suspected, Marcus had a superb whole-floor apartment in an exclusive complex right on the beach. There were only nine apartments and Marcus lived in the penthouse. A private elevator took them with their bags right up to the front door, although Marcus indicated he often made use of the stairs for the exercise.

The intricately carved front door was impressive enough, but as Laura followed him inside she caught her breath as he flipped the light on. The effects of the air-con were already evident. Marcus walked over to press a button, to allow the blinds to slide open on the balcony doors. Pausing in the main lounge area, she took in the expanse of the apartment. Everywhere she looked there were elegant shades of blue and grey. The tiled foyer gave way to a thick grey carpet flecked with blue. A dark-grey leather lounge suite dominated one corner of the room. At the far end, a more informal area flowed onto the balcony. Three steps led up to a large separate dining room with big picture windows that, when the vertical blinds were opened, would reveal the Pacific Ocean—the ever-changing colours of the sea a perfect foil for formal meals. The sleek grey table would easily seat a dozen guests. The kitchen, also set in tones of blue and grey, was huge, with an island bench. Masculine, yet very functional. Once again, the kitchen had water views. The casual eating area was smaller, with a round six-seater table. A sliding door, of course, led to another balcony. Everything was designed to take maximum advantage of the ocean views.

Laura followed Marcus through the darkened interior of the apartment, stopping only when he opened a door to a guest room. He left her to settle in. The first thing she did was to open the dark curtains to allow the afternoon light in. Then, unable to resist, she unlocked the catch to the sliding door and stepped out onto her own private balcony. There was a small square table at one end with a matching chair. The tang of the ocean spray greeted her as the breeze gently rustled the hem of her floral sundress. She leaned against the railing, breathing deeply, and felt the tension of the last few weeks subside.

Reluctantly, she turned back inside and began to unpack her things. The room was on the large side, but comfortable. The double bed boasted a blue and white geometric cover, with half a dozen pillows arranged at the head. There was a built-in wardrobe with sliding doors. Thankfully, the doors were not mirrored. An expensive looking armchair sat between the bed and the sliding glass door, with a small timber side table nearby.

An ensuite bathroom in the palest blue tonings was set off by darker blue towels hanging on the double towel rail.

A short time later, she emerged to scan the rest of the apartment. There was another bedroom similar to hers next door, and on the other side of it, a study. A large, high-backed swivel office chair was pushed back from the heavily carved wooden desk, but with its back to the window behind. Floor-to-ceiling bookcases lined one wall. Beside them, three heavy filing cabinets, one of which she noted on closer inspection was reserved entirely for Medi-Aid. The other two were for work and personal use respectively.

She startled as Marcus opened the door between his bedroom and the study, seemingly unconcerned to find her there. He picked up his briefcase from the floor near the bedroom door, walked over and swung it onto the desktop.

"This place is pretty impressive," she told him.

He glanced up at her as he opened the lid and pulled out papers. "It's home. Do you like it?"

"Yes, from what I've seen so far."

"Have a wander around," he told her, indicating the door to his bedroom.

She hesitated, but curiosity got the better of her and she walked through into the other room. Once again, blue dominated, as bold and as confident as the man himself. This time the king-sized bed was covered in rich blue with white accents. Marc's duffle bag was open on the bed with the contents strewn around. The door to the walk-in robe was open and the light was on. All his clothes were neatly arranged. Although blues dominated, there was a good mix of other colours in his wardrobe. She stuck her head into the massive ensuite bathroom that continued the rich blue tones. A raised spa bath took up one corner and a large twin shower the other. A double vanity and bench ran the length of one wall with ample cupboard space beneath. The wall above was mirrored, with three separate wood-framed panels. Continuing to the sliding door to his balcony, she knew the view from this bedroom would be just as impressive as the other rooms.

On the way back through the apartment she passed a storeroom, a utility room, and what she assumed was the laundry area. Everything was secreted behind closed doors.

Marcus had opened up the apartment and, in the light, his place appeared even more impressive. She found him out on the balcony off the casual dining area, leaning up against the rail as she had done earlier. His sleeves were rolled-up and the top couple of buttons of his shirt undone. She could see him relax visibly as he savoured the view.

He turned to Laura as she joined him at the railing.

"Do you ever tire of it?"

"No, never. I'm a real beach boy. I don't think I could live anywhere else for long."

"So that's why you chose to do work with Medi-Aid on a tropical island, not some landlocked country in the middle of Africa."

He chuckled. "Sprung. You're right. I need to be near the water as much as possible."

"Aren't you concerned about the possibilities of cyclones up here?"

"It's the price I'm prepared to pay in order to have these views." He indicated the expanse of water.

"I don't imagine there's anything in the way of surf, though."

"No, the Great Barrier Reef puts paid to that, but that's okay."

"What about stingers?"

"They're around from about November until March, so I just wear a stinger suit."

"Well, I have to admit it's pretty spectacular."

"Wait till you've seen the ocean in all its moods. Everything is so much more dramatic up here. Some days the water is as smooth as glass, it's so tranquil and peaceful, and then a storm whips up angry grey seas. It foams and swirls and hurls itself against the beach. You learn to appreciate all its various guises and all it has to offer… rather like some women I've known."

He caught her eyes for what seemed like an eternity, but it was probably all of a couple of seconds. Something flickered in the chocolate depths and he just wanted to dive in headfirst. It took a lot of effort to tear himself away and leave her to enjoy the view.

❧

"Fancy something to eat?" he asked as she ventured inside a short time later. He'd already changed into tan chinos and a pale green polo shirt.

"What are you offering? Baked beans? Two-minute noodles?"

"Why don't you have a look in the fridge." He heard her gasp as she saw the contents, and answered her questioning look. "I rang ahead and asked my housekeeper to stock up. How about some pasta?"

"Sure, are you cooking, or am I?"

"My place, I'll cook. I'll have you know I can rustle up a pretty mean primavera."

"You like to cook then?"

He made a face. "I do, but I have to confess I don't always have time, especially when I have a heavy operating schedule. It's much easier to come home to a prepared meal. Mrs Knight, bless her, is as good as a cordon bleu chef."

Laura felt awkward just standing around. She was relieved when Marcus put her to work preparing the salad.

❧

"That was delicious, thank you," she told him as they adjourned to the balcony later.

He was chuffed she liked his cooking. After a few minutes of small talk, they lapsed into companionable silence. He watched as she leaned back in her chair and closed her eyes, listening no doubt to the sound of the waves as they crept up the beach.

He leaned towards her, desperate to feel the softness of her lips once more, but pulled back. "Can I interest you in a beach walk in the moonlight?" He knew it was probably a long shot, but he needed to ask anyway. Laura was slow to answer, and he guessed she was weighing up the offer, but he was willing her to say yes.

"Um… no… I don't think I could be bothered getting up… thanks all the same… but I'm happy just to sit here."

Marcus didn't think he could continue to sit there with her without— He got up, disappointed that she wouldn't be joining him. "I could do with a walk, so I'll see you a bit later."

She was already settling back when he left.

The floodlights from the apartment building, along with the moon, cast enough light for him to see his way onto the sand. The beach was his relaxation spot, his contemplative place. Where he could unwind after a hectic day. Where he could regain his equilibrium, his peace, and settle his mind.

But not tonight. His thoughts were swirling all over the place. He had thought he could handle the whole fake engagement thing without getting caught up. Now he wasn't so sure. Laura. She was getting under his skin. Every day, she was drawing him a little further in, not that she noticed.

Would she fit into his world here in the far north of the state? Would she get along with his friends and family? What was he even thinking, bringing her up here in the first place? What if she decided to call him out in front of the people he cared about the most? She wouldn't, would she? She had gone along with it all so far. But then, pretending in front of strangers was a whole lot easier.

If he was honest with himself, he wasn't pretending so much anymore. He was really falling for her, and he had no idea how she felt about him. Sometimes, he'd catch her off-guard and there would be something there in her eyes that made him think that maybe, just maybe, she was starting to develop some emotional connection. But who was he kidding? Nothing Laura had said or done had ever given any indication she felt something brewing between them.

CHAPTER SIXTEEN

Laura's next test in Cairns was to meet the other doctors Marcus worked with at the Calvary Medical Centre, a stone's throw from the hospital of the same name. His late-model BMW convertible was, of course, blue—midnight blue, to be precise. She could tell he enjoyed the handling of the car as they sped along the highway, back into Cairns where his "reserved" underground parking space was waiting.

This morning, he had morphed into the very epitome of a young, successful surgeon, with expensive tailored trousers and a pale blue shirt rolled up to the elbow, no tie—which she guessed was a small concession to the tropical heat. The cheap plastic watch he'd been wearing had been replaced by a blue-faced Rolex, with an elegant yellow-gold and stainless-steel band. And who knew how much product he'd used to get his hair to sit perfectly? Thankfully for her own hair, he hadn't lowered the roof of the car.

Laura hesitated, sucking in a deep breath and steeling herself before following her "fiancé" into the building. The relatively new medical centre housed General Practitioners on the first floor with specialists on the second level. Surrounded by well-established trees, the building was virtually invisible from the road. They took the elevator up to the second floor. There was so much light flooding into the building from the huge windows, there wasn't much need for artificial light. Light reached even the bottom level from a central atrium protected by a railing. As she looked down, Laura noticed an internal garden with seating downstairs. A few people were taking advantage of the tranquil spot.

Everyone they came across, from other doctors to receptionists and cleaners, seemed genuinely pleased to see Marcus again. He stopped to have a few words with each of them, introducing her as well.

She had been unsure what to wear for the occasion, settling for a lightweight sleeveless white sundress with a scattering of red flowers around the hem.

The glass-fronted reception area for the suite of rooms Marcus shared with Doctor Roger Lambert held a small indoor garden complete with miniature waterfall and fishpond. The room was empty, apart from a lone woman on the desk. In her late fifties, she seemed at first glance to be the personification of an efficient, no-nonsense receptionist, wearing a navy blouse with small white polka dots. Her dark hair was short and businesslike. She peered over the top of her glasses, beaming when she recognised her boss.

"Marcus, good to see you back."

He walked around the counter and accepted her warm hug. "Not for long, I'm afraid. Life for the time being is governed by speaking and fundraising engagements. Still, it's all in a good cause." He turned to Laura. "Ellen, I'd like you to meet my fiancée, Laura Maxwell. No doubt you have been reading all about her."

Laura could tell she was being assessed to see if she was a suitable partner for the good doctor, but she was unsure if she had passed muster. Ellen Wagner was polite enough, but there was an undercurrent evident in her manner.

Laura mentioned it to Marc when they were in the sanctuary of his consultation room.

"She's just being protective," he assured her. "Likes to do the mothering bit. Probably miffed because she didn't get the first chance of approval."

Laura sat down while he flicked through some of the papers in his in-tray. The room was sparsely decorated. Grey desk and bookshelves set off by a couple of tropical beach prints. A Lladro figurine of a surgeon in green scrubs perched on one corner of the desk. The desktop was clear, apart from a phone and a small pad of pathology referral slips. The blue-topped examination table to the right was behind the main door, out of the direct line of vision from the waiting room. The pale grey curtain that hung between the table and the small sink was tied back. The door to an adjoining second consultation room was slightly ajar, and Laura figured it would probably be a mirror image of the room she was in now.

A few minutes later, she walked with him to the staff common room that served the entire upper floor. Apparently all the partners with their different specialties took the opportunity to touch base with one another, which could not have been easy given their hectic schedules. Two figures stood as they entered, and greeted Marcus with enthusiasm.

A tall, thin, dark-haired surgeon introduced himself. "Doctor Roger Lambert. Pleased to meet you. Laura, isn't it?"

"Yes, that's right… you went to med school with Marcus, didn't you?"

He nodded as he shook her hand.

"And I'm Gail Peterson," the petite redhead beside him interrupted.

"Gail is one of our paediatricians," Marcus told Laura. They chatted for a few minutes before Gail excused herself. Roger Lambert busied himself making a cup of coffee as more doctors arrived.

"Ah, Bradley, it's about time you brought yer lassie to meet us."

Laura turned to greet the owner of the Scottish lilt. He took her hand and lightly kissed the top of it.

"Doctor Alex McGregor at your service, Ms Maxwell. The newspaper photos don't do you justice, hey Bradley? You certainly landed a stunner, laddie." The charming tow-headed Scotsman weaved some magic with his words, all the while teasing his friend and partner.

"Okay, McGregor, that's enough of your sweet talk." Marcus introduced Laura to the other doctors as they came and went as news spread of Marc's return.

"Well, I think you've met everyone. Except for Susan, but I'm sure she will be here before too long." After some small talk, the others drifted away. As he fixed himself a mug of coffee, Marcus filled her in about his work colleagues. She remembered some of them from her discussions with Marc back in the jungle. It was good to put a face to the names.

Without warning, the door burst open and a blonde dynamo exploded into the room.

"Marc, I just heard you were back, it's good to see you, you look great, how are you?" Her questions rolled into each other. She quickly closed the gap and reached up to give him a resounding kiss. Marcus lent down to hug her and turned her around to Laura. They looked like they were on very friendly terms. A major stab of jealousy hit Laura unexpectedly. Was she a former girlfriend? Was he still interested in her? It sure seemed like it.

"Laura, this is our obstetrician/gynaecologist, Susan Clarke—"

"Walsh," she corrected him. "I'm married now remember."

Letting go of a breath she didn't realise she had been holding, a relieved Laura watched with interest as the interaction between Susan and Marcus played out.

"Oh yeah, how could I forget. Poor Tim, how is he coping with you?"

Susan promptly elbowed him in the ribs at which he pretended to double up in pain, but Susan took no notice.

"Actually," she winked at Laura, "I gave up waiting for Doctor Bradley to propose, so I found someone else… Laura, isn't it? I'm thrilled someone has finally been able to pin him down." Susan threw a glance back over her shoulder at him. "We were all secretly despairing of Marcus finding someone to share his life with. However did you manage it?"

Laura just shrugged.

Susan checked her wristwatch. "Have you had lunch yet by any chance?"

"No… er… actually I haven't."

"Good, well I'm going over the road, there's a lovely little café, would you like to come along?"

"Yeah sure, thanks."

"You'll have to excuse me, ladies," Marc said, draining his mug. "Roger would like another opinion about a patient he's operating on this afternoon. I'd like to go over the case history with him."

"Heck, Marc, you weren't even invited."

He just shook his head in mock despair, kissing Laura lightly on the cheek. "Have fun."

THE TWO WOMEN walked out of the air-conditioned building into the warmth of the tropical sun. Susan talked non-stop as they crossed the grassed area beside the medical centre and joined the path that took them to the kerbside. Susan pressed the walk button and kept talking as they waited for the lights to change. As Laura followed, Susan veered off down a laneway and ducked into a small café about halfway down. It was like they had been transported back to the 1940s. A typical old-style

Greek café if ever she saw one. The old weathered sign that hung on the wall behind the counter proclaimed it to be Nicoli's Bakery and she wondered if it was still in Greek hands. From the greeting Susan gave, Laura thought it might well be.

"Hello Doctor Walsh, can I get you your regular?"

"Sure Dimitri, thanks so much."

"What about your friend?"

"Just give her a minute to have a look."

"Let me know when you are ready to order then."

Laura nodded as she ran an eye over the glass-fronted counter that held a tantalising display of cakes and slices.

Slipping into the booth seat across from Susan, towards the back of the café, Laura picked up a menu, perused the list and made her choice.

"So how did you two meet, again?" Susan asked.

"In the hospital on Levati. I had been there a couple of weeks before he arrived."

"Love at first sight, huh?"

"Not exactly," Laura admitted.

"Well, looks like it all happened pretty fast then. Marc was still very much a confirmed bachelor when he left here. We're all in a bit of shock, to say the least. It's so out of character for him, must have fallen hard and fast. Still when you know... you know."

"You said you gave up waiting for him to propose. How long were you two in a relationship?"

Susan laughed. "I was just teasing. We have only ever been good friends. Sure, we dated once or twice a couple of years back, but we quickly came to the conclusion that we were just destined to be friends." She paused before continuing. "So, what is it about Doctor Bradley that made you realise he was the one?"

Laura had worried this might happen. She had no idea how to answer, to keep her companion happy without actually coming right out and lying.

She took her time, hoping she looked like there was so much about him she liked that she didn't know where to start. "Um… there wasn't any one thing in particular, just a number of things that when they all added up meant…." She trailed off and just shrugged, hoping she looked soft and gooey and totally in love with the man.

After the meal arrived, Susan went on to tell a few stories about Marc and then started on how she met her husband.

Although Laura could hardly get a word in edgewise, she was drawn to Susan. By the end of a very long lunch they had become firm friends. Laura was invited to dinner, along with Marcus.

"Sorry, we'll have to take a raincheck. Marcus is driving me up to the Daintree tomorrow to meet his family."

"No worries, we'll catch up some other time," Susan told her cheerfully. "I guess I had better get back and do some work. Reports, what fun."

Marcus looked up from his paperwork when Laura put her head around the door. "How was lunch?"

"Yeah, good thanks."

"Did you get on alright with Susan?"

"You'd have to be a pretty hard case not to get on with Susan."

He chuckled. "I guess so. I'm about done here, so we can go if you like."

Laura nodded and waited for him to join her. He said goodbye to his receptionist on the way out. Laura still thought Ellen disapproved of her.

On the drive back, Marcus told her about a change in their plans.

"I'll be assisting Roger Lambert in theatre tomorrow morning. I still hope we can get away later in the afternoon, but I'll try and let you know how things are going. Are you okay with that?"

She nodded. What did it matter anyway? It was his show.

BY THE TIME Marcus arrived back at the apartment the next day, it was mid-afternoon. The operation, although a lengthy, difficult procedure, had gone well. Laura assumed he would appreciate a rest before heading off, but he was keen to get going. Soon after he'd showered and changed, they were on the road north.

She glanced sideways as they travelled. Marcus was dressed in cocoa-coloured shorts and a butter-yellow shirt. His tan was beginning to darken again, and the shirt he wore emphasised it. Strong hands rested lightly on the steering wheel, tapping a finger to the beat of the music playing on the CD player. He had wide-ranging musical tastes. She recalled some of the, at times heated, discussions they'd had about various recording artists back in the Levati jungle hut. Currently, there was an instrumental jazz album playing. The further they drove, the more relaxed he seemed to become. She, on the other hand, was getting more and more nervous.

CHAPTER SEVENTEEN

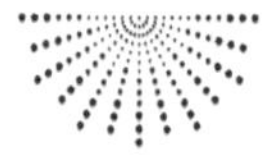

*D*avid Bradley's home literally backed onto the rainforest. It was well hidden, off a quiet lane some distance from the main road through town. As the BMW drew to a stop, Laura pulled down the visor to use the mirror to check her appearance. She had decided to wear long white dress shorts with a wide, tan leather belt and teamed it with a white singlet top under an ice pink blouse which tied at the waist. She was worried about the impression she would make and hadn't realised she had voiced her thoughts until Marcus told her to relax as he opened the car door for her.

"He'll be as captivated as I was the first time I saw you."

Laura wasn't sure she'd heard him properly. He launched himself up the front stairs of the highset Queenslander three at a time, waiting at the top for her to catch up before crossing the wide veranda to lift the brass door knocker.

The instant the door opened, Laura knew how Marcus would look thirty years from now. Doctor Bradley senior had the same good looks, matured over time. The hair was still thick, although grey, and the vivid blue eyes were encircled by wire rimmed spectacles. A tad shorter than his son, he was wearing a blue plaid short-sleeved button-down shirt with black chinos and casual slip on shoes. The years had been kind. He was a very handsome man.

"Marcus, my boy, good to see you in the flesh at last." Father and son embraced warmly.

David Bradley turned his attention to the slim figure beside his youngest son.

"Dad, this is Laura. Laura, this is my father, Doctor David Bradley." He put an arm around her as Laura shook the older man's hand.

"My dear, I'm pleased to finally be able to meet you. Marcus has told me so much about you over the phone."

Laura was slightly stunned at this revelation as she was pulled into an affectionate embrace. She had no idea Marcus had even talked to his father. But then, why wouldn't he? They seemed to have a close relationship. How on earth was she going to be able to convince the older man they were a couple. Surely, he would be able to see right through the charade.

"Come in, come in. You must be about ready for a long cool drink." She noticed the gold signet ring on his right hand, with a red gem in place of the blue one on Marc's ring she was wearing. Maybe it was a male Bradley thing.

Laura sat next to Marcus as he related details of the morning's operation to his father. Barely listening, she took in her surroundings. It was a beautiful modern take on a traditional Queenslander, built high to take advantage of any breeze. The house was a showpiece of the best of Australian timbers. Everywhere you looked were magnificent textures and grains. The floors were highly polished. Bookcases lined one wall in the lounge area. Laura remembered Marcus telling her his parents had the house designed and built almost fifteen years ago as a quiet retreat from the demands of their respective jobs. His as a highly regarded neurosurgeon, and hers as a much loved and very popular General Practitioner. It was here that David Bradley nursed his wife through the last days of her battle with cancer.

The conversation eventually turned to Levati and all the details surrounding their kidnap. Marcus had evidently spoken to his father at length on the phone. He knew most of what had gone on, but David Bradley was keen to hear about the ordeal from Laura's point of view. She'd gone over the story so many times now she could recite it in her sleep, but with Marc's father she could share a bit more than she would dare with most people.

He was as easy to talk to as his son.

LAURA'S ROOM was beautifully furnished. A huge carved colonial bed dominated the room, covered in a handmade quilt in soft pinks. Laura spent a long time examining the hand piecing. His mother's hobby, she remembered. Obviously made with so much love.

There was a matching blanket box at the foot of the bed, its rich tapestry-covered lid resplendent in pink and burgundy roses. An old washstand stood nearby, complete with a matching pitcher and basin. A soft, fluffy pink towel lay folded with a bar of guest soap nestled in its folds.

Laura turned the key of the massive wardrobe that stood near the French window and unpacked her few belongings. She was quick to tie back the floor length curtains and open the doors to let in some of the tropical breeze.

MUCH LATER, she dressed for dinner in a short black dress with a sweetheart neckline, capped sleeves and a lace skirt. After surveying her upswept hair, Laura wandered along the length of the veranda, dropping her purse on a chair by the lounge door. It was so quiet and tranquil. A place to relax and restore the soul. A perfect getaway for the medicos who had built it.

Stretching her arms out along the rail, she inhaled deeply and listened to the rainforest sounds.

SHE WASN'T in her room when he knocked. Walking to the lounge area, he spotted a figure out at the rail. Laura. As he walked to the doorway, his breath hitched at the sight of her in the knee-length, flirty black dress. Her hair was pinned up. It looked elegant, but he much preferred it down, and debated if he could get away with pulling it free.

Standing quietly, he drank her in as she stretched and leaned forward slightly. *Don't scare her, Bradley.* Knowing full well if he set one foot on the veranda he would be in all sorts of trouble, he went anyway. *Look, don't touch*, he warned himself—to no avail. He slipped his left arm around her and rested it lightly on the rail under her outstretched arm.

LAURA WAS CAUGHT OFF-GUARD. Normally she had enough time to prime her body not to react to his nearness. Her heart rate increased, her breathing quickened, and she chided herself for her automatic response. He stood barely a centimetre away and she could feel the surge of awareness at the warmth of his breath on her neck as his words brushed her cheek. "It's very peaceful here, isn't it?"

She nodded, not game to move—not that she could have, even if she wanted to. And there was no way she wanted to. She drew in a delicate breath to inhale his scent.

The light from the lounge room spilled into the dark of the gathering night, pooling at her feet. He put his free hand on her waist. When it started to move slowly down over her hips, she grabbed his wrist to stop him. He bent his head and kissed the bare nape of her neck. Laura couldn't suppress the shiver that danced down her spine.

～

Sensing her pliancy, Marcus turned her gently and claimed her lips. A small groan escaped her as he pulled her closer and deepened the kiss. His hands easily moulded her body against the firmness of his own. He closed his eyes to savour every bit of her. Her sweet scent was driving him crazy.

She responded. He felt her hands as they crept up the crisp material of his white shirt and burnt through the fabric.

～

Just as well he had a firm hold on her. She was suddenly incapable of standing on her own feet. She enjoyed the feel of his muscled chest. The rapid rate of his heartbeat was evident to her manicured fingertips as they rested lightly on his upper torso.

He lifted his head slightly and, cradling her face in one hand, brushed his thumb over the soft fullness of her lips. In the semi-darkness, his eyes were huge, seeking hers.

"See what an effect you have on me," he told her huskily, before kissing a trail of fire from her ear to her neck and back across her lips.

Playing the publicity game was evidently becoming increasingly difficult for him, as it was for Laura. She wrapped her hands around his neck and pulled him closer to her lips. She couldn't get enough and threatened to self-destruct. He tasted so good. Smelled even better. She willingly allowed his tongue to dip into her mouth. Was that her low throaty groan, or was it his? She couldn't be sure, maybe it was both of them?

The feelings she had for Marcus Bradley were growing deeper, despite her best efforts to keep her emotions at bay. This was supposed to be nothing more than a fake relationship with a use-by date somewhere down the track. She was beginning to wonder if the use-by date could be extended somehow.

An apologetic cough from the doorway finally drew them apart.

"I'm… er… sorry to interrupt… but our dinner reservations are for 7.30."

Marcus nodded as his father disappeared back inside the house. Laura followed wordlessly, picking up her purse. Marcus allowed her enough time to repair her makeup.

"You'd better get in the front," he told her quietly, opening the door of his father's Mercedes, "or I won't be able to keep my hands off you."

Positive her cheeks were as red as the car's paintwork, she climbed in next to David Bradley, but he seemed not to have heard.

The exclusive restaurant nestled easily into the rainforest. A glass wall at the back allowed diners visual access to the gardens outside, glowing from the soft lighting set amongst the dark green of the foliage. Guests could also eat outside on the deck area, overlooking the manicured garden with its mini waterfall and bush timber seating. Laura could imagine it would be a popular wedding venue.

Marc's father was obviously a regular diner. Many people, staff and patrons alike, greeted him by name.

They were led to a secluded table alongside the glass feature wall. The candlelit table reflected off the glass as they ate. Doctor Bradley senior soon had her at ease, and they conversed on a wide range of topics.

The grilled chicken breast fillet she chose had a simple citrus marinade. It was delectable, and Laura was quick to send her compliments to the chef. Both men chose to enjoy the grilled barramundi. For dessert, Laura could not help herself. Triple layer pavlova with passionfruit and mango curd. The soft centre of a pavlova with a crispy outer shell never failed to delight her.

Goodness, this one was divine. Topped with generous ribbon swirls of mango flesh and passionfruit. It was amazing, right down to the last bite. Reluctantly, she shared a spoonful with Marcus and was rewarded with a taste of his mango lime tart.

MARCUS HAD BEEN ABOUT to feed her the dessert morsel, but with his father nearby he decided it would be safer to let her take the spoon for herself. He couldn't help but watch as she lifted the spoon to her mouth. Wishing they were alone, he barely restrained himself from leaning over to get a taste of mango and lime from her lips, convinced it would taste much better that way.

During coffee, David Bradley pushed a small black box across the table to his son. Marcus flipped the lid to reveal a signet ring, identical to the one she was now wearing as a fake engagement ring.

Marcus appreciated his father's gesture, and smoothly slipped the family crest onto his little finger. "Thanks, Dad. I must admit, it took a while to get used to not having it on." He looked over to Laura. "I'd been wearing that one since I was seventeen."

"YOU SHOULD HAVE SAID SOMETHING, Marc. I would have gladly given it back."

He shook his head. "I was more than happy to give you something that means so much to me." Picking up her left hand and raising it to his mouth, he kissed her fingers lightly.

The warmth in his blue eyes invaded her soul and confused her. She dropped her gaze, unable to cope with the depth of emotion she saw reflected, mirroring the strength of her own feelings.

Laura was subdued later on the way back to the house, and excused herself as soon as possible. "I'm sure you two have a lot to catch up on. I'm pretty tired, so I'm going to call it a night."

She reached up to kiss Marcus briefly on the cheek before escaping to her room. After getting ready for the night, she sat on the edge of her bed for a long time. The dynamics of her relationship with Marcus were changing.

Unsure if he was playing the part to the hilt or whether it might be for real, Laura had determined to keep herself at a distance emotionally—but it was getting harder each day.

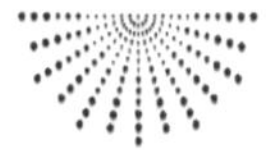

CHAPTER EIGHTEEN

*D*ressed in a blue-print halter-neck maxi dress, Laura left her hair untied and went downstairs to meet Marc's brother and his family.

The lunchtime barbecue was a chance for Stephen and Danielle to see Marcus and finally meet Laura. They had flown to Cairns from Townsville for the weekend and driven a hire car to the Bradley home.

After the initial hubbub died down, she wandered over to the group standing in the entertainment area under the house, while David Bradley prepared to fire up the barbecue. She caught sight of Marc's slight nod of approval as he reached out to take her hand and pull her to his side.

"Laura, I'd like you to meet my brother Stephen and his wife Danielle. Guys, this is Laura."

She shook hands with Stephen, who was fractionally taller than Marcus with similar smouldering good looks. It was easy to tell they were brothers, although Stephen had brown hair and eyes. Laura knew from the photos on the living room wall upstairs that Stephen favoured their mother more, with her dark eyes and olive complexion. Danielle's hair also was dark blonde and she had striking green eyes. She wore black capri pants and a bright flowing tropical-print kaftan top.

"I see he's got you doing it already," Stephen said by way of introduction.

"Doing what?" Laura asked, puzzled.

"Wearing blue." He grinned. "Sometimes I think my brother would like to see everyone in blue. He tends to forget there are other colours in the spectrum." Stephen pointed a finger at his younger brother's choice of shirt: sky blue.

"There's a shade of blue to suit everyone," Marcus replied good naturedly.

"No thanks, give me red any day." His brother indicated his own open-necked red shirt.

Danielle took it upon herself to interrupt. "Just ignore them, they are always having a spat about something." Both men shrugged their shoulders with mock indignation and changed the subject.

Just then, three children hurtled around the side of the house.

"Woah, slow down a minute," Stephen called as they cut through the barbecue area. All three skidded to a halt. "What's the rule about running near the barbecue?"

"But Dad!" all three protested.

"Come on, you have plenty of other places to run. Now before you take off again, I'd like you to come and meet Laura." He looked down at them. "Ah… no grumbling, you'll be free in a minute. Laura, I'd like you to meet our children. This is Luke, Ashlee and Jacinta."

Luke, tall for his age and dressed in shorts and a North Queensland Cowboys shirt, was like his father, with the same brown eyes—which were currently scowling. The girls were mini blonde versions of their mother, each with long hair tied back in a ponytail. One girl was dressed in a lilac shirt. The other twin was wearing a checked blouse.

Marc pretended he didn't know which twin was which. "So, this is Ashlee," he said, gesturing to one of the girls, "and this is Jacinta." He put his hands on his hips looking down at them both. "Then again, maybe this one is Jacinta and this one is Ashlee." He crossed his arms pointing the other way. "I don't know who is who."

He winked at Laura as he dropped to his haunches and pretended to look closer. He grabbed the closest niece and pretended to inspect her closely as she dissolved into fits of giggles. "Well you look like you could be Jacinta but maybe you're not…" He looked from one to the other in mock confusion. The girls laughed and rolled their eyes at him.

"Uncle Marc," they groaned in unison. "Remember the freckle?"

"Oh… that's right… come to think of it, one of them does have a freckle on her neck. But I don't remember which one." More eye rolling.

"That's me, Ashlee." She pointed at the spot on her neck just above her left collarbone. It was tiny, so Laura couldn't see it from where she stood—she'd just have to take their word for it.

"Oh, so it is." He reached for them both. "So, if you're Ashlee, that means you are… ticklish!" He grabbed Jacinta and started to make her laugh. As Ashlee tried to save her sibling she was also tickled.

It was a few minutes before they all caught their breath. Marcus stood with one twin on either side and brought them to Laura.

"Hi girls," she said, "it's good to meet you in person. Your Uncle Marc has told me so much about you."

Luke wasn't impressed with all the fuss, she could tell. He shuffled his sneakers on the floor.

"Remember I said Laura is going to marry Uncle Marcus," their father told them.

The twins' faces lit up. "Really?" they chorused. Luke just shoved his hands into the pockets of his shorts.

"Could we be in the wedding?" the girls asked.

"We'd be good flower girls."

"We could wear beautiful long pink dresses," Ashlee sighed.

Her sister nudged her. "Or we could wear blue if you want, Uncle Marc." She flashed her green eyes at him.

He just laughed and ruffled her hair. "Pink will be fine, girls."

Ashlee and Jacinta squealed and hugged each other excitedly.

"We're going to be flower girls!!" they said, over and over, jumping up and down.

"Hey Mum, did you hear that?" Jacinta shouted. "We're going to be flower girls at Uncle Marc's wedding."

Danielle intercepted the surprised look Laura threw Marcus as the twins darted away with their brother. She took Laura's arm.

"You don't have to have the girls in the wedding party if you have someone else in mind."

"No, it's not that," Laura replied, casting around for a suitable explanation. "It's um… just that we haven't set a date yet and, well… they might drive you up the wall between now and then." She knew Marcus was listening in to the conversation. "Really, I'd be happy to have the twins as flower girls."

"Are you sure?"

Laura nodded, hoping she didn't appear the fraud she felt. She was relieved when it was announced that the food was ready.

MARCUS KNEW his brother had been keen to meet Laura in person.

Stephen had seen the stories and photos and of course spoken to Marcus on the phone, but he had wanted to see for himself the person who had managed to capture his younger brother's interest. She was a little reserved initially, which was understandable given that she was meeting "the family" for the first time. But as she gradually started to relax, he and Danielle found Laura charming and she won over the twins.

He pulled Marcus aside later. "Laura gets the tick of approval from both of us," Stephen told his sibling. "Make sure you look after her."

"Thanks, I will."

Despite some early misgivings, Laura found the extended Bradley family wonderful to get along with—friendly and easy-going. Laura was able to relax and enjoy their company. Marcus, as usual, played his part to perfection. An affectionate and loving fiancé. She responded in kind, but she wasn't really acting her role anymore. Well, up to a certain point. She didn't want to give her emotions free rein, lest Marcus found out the truth of her feelings towards him.

It wasn't until later, after the others had left, that she felt a growing sense of disquiet.

His family had loved her as Marcus knew they would. But Laura seemed distant. She had busied herself with the dishes. He tossed a tea towel at her to try and get her attention.

"Hey, you're very quiet all of a sudden. What's up?"

"Nothing."

He wasn't convinced. "Laura?" He waited as she bit her lip and glanced around to see if they were alone. David Bradley was busy on the phone in his study.

"It's your family," she finally admitted.

"What about them?"

"I like them a lot."

"So, why so glum?"

She dropped her gaze. "I um… just feel really guilty about

lying to them about our relationship. I'm here under false pretences. I feel terrible about making plans to have your nieces as flower girls when there isn't even going to be a wedding. It's not so bad pretending in front of people who don't know you at all… but family and friends… They are going to be so shocked when we pull the plug on this. The twins will be devastated."

"Let's not cross that bridge until we come to it."

Silence.

"Laura." He put a finger under her chin and forced her gaze up to his. "As far as everyone is concerned, we're happily engaged. In fact, you almost had me convinced there this afternoon."

She shrugged at him. "I'm getting used to playing the part. It's almost second nature now."

"You might get an Academy Award yet."

She slipped out of his grasp and returned to the job at hand. "Well you wouldn't be far behind."

"I guess not. I must admit it is becoming a bit of a grind."

It was the first indicator Laura had received from Marcus that he wasn't totally enjoying his role. "Why don't you call a halt to it all?"

"If it wasn't for all the publicity, I'd have chucked it in long ago. But donations have been coming in at a phenomenal rate and we need all the funds we can get. Who knows how long the public fascination with us will last? We have to take advantage of it while we can."

He put the last of the dishes away and hung up the tea towel. "Every time I'm tempted to quit, I just think of all those children on Levati, with families who are relying on us to help them because there is no one else, and it gives me enough incentive to keep going for a while longer."

That, and the fact he couldn't bear the thought of them going their separate ways. He should tell her, but he couldn't… just yet.

~

So, there it was, Laura thought in her room later. Marcus found the whole charade laborious. *What had you hoped for?* she mocked herself, after she climbed into bed. That he would say everything had been worthwhile because he had met her? That he was deeply in love with her and needed to spend as much time with her as possible? That he couldn't stand to be away from her?

Get real, Laura, he's just playing the part. Albeit in a totally convincing manner. She'd almost believed him herself. But she knew it was all part of the publicity charade and, as long as the public were believing them and lapping it up, he was more than happy to give them what they wanted.

The knowledge that her feelings were one-sided wasn't as devastating a discovery as she initially feared, and she vowed not to give Marcus any indication of her true feelings—they would all have to stay under lock and key.

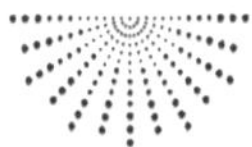

CHAPTER NINETEEN

"How would you feel about going back to Levati?" Marcus looked up as he put the phone receiver down.

"What do you mean, go back?"

"That was Mike Martin's producer. They want to know if they can do a follow-up story and film us going back to Levati." He watched the colour drain from her face.

"I'm not keen, to be honest." She sat down opposite him quickly, as if she had been winded.

"We wouldn't go back to the trouble spots. They would be prepared to get the US Army on board to help out and provide an escort. It would only be for a couple of days. A bit of film at the hospital and then at the clinic... and at the army base."

"It's a long way to go for a couple of days' filming."

"That's what they want to do."

"Who would be coming, then?"

"A camera crew, the producer and Mike Martin. Apparently, he wants to do the story himself. It would be great publicity for Medi-Aid, Laura."

Her head was down as she bit her lip. "Couldn't you just go? Wouldn't that be enough?"

"It has to be both of us. You know that."

"Oh Marc, it's too soon, I don't think I could cope just yet."

"Laura, we would be perfectly safe. A camera crew and the might of the US Army as an armed escort. Confronting the memories will do you— both of us good. Help us to move on."

He felt a huge amount of guilt for pushing her to go. Quite apart from the publicity it would generate, he genuinely felt she needed to face Levati to help give her some peace of mind. Dialling the number he'd written down, he spoke to the show's producer to confirm they would go ahead with the trip, all the while keeping an eye on Laura who was seemingly frozen in her chair. Lost somewhere in her memories of Levati, no doubt.

"Well, that's settled." He put the phone down again. "They will make all the arrangements and let us know the dates." Marcus walked around to where she was sitting and got down on his haunches in front of her. "Laura, it will be okay. Nothing bad will happen, I promise."

IF ONLY SHE could believe those words. Shaking her head, she fled the room, needing to get out. Suffocating. The walls were closing in. She didn't want to be trapped and needed to move. Quickly. Out, down the stairs, across to the sand.

Within a few paces, the smell of the salt air had calmed her somewhat. The light breeze picked up her hair and blew it across her face. Pulling it back behind her head as she walked, Laura tried to come to terms with returning to Levati. Could she do it? Did she even want to go back there again? The nightmares hadn't abated. What if she saw one of their captors again? What if… ?

She wasn't sure she could go back, despite Marc's assurances they'd be perfectly safe. Then again, if the US Army were on their side, surely they'd be okay—wouldn't they?

~

AND SO, a mere ten days later she was shaking hands with Mike Martin at the airport. "The" Mike Martin, in the flesh. She'd practically grown up watching him on television. He was a well-respected journalist and had interviewed many famous people over the years, from heads of state to movie stars to regular mums and dads with a compelling story to tell. A genuinely nice bloke. The producer introduced herself and the rest of the crew —the cameraman and sound recordist.

They tried to put her at ease but the whole trip still daunted her, and it started at the customs counter. "Ms Maxwell, just a reminder that you will need to get your passport renewed. You'll just scrape in this time, but don't forget you need at least six months left on your passport to travel to most places overseas."

"Oh, okay. Thanks for pointing that out."

At least they got to travel business class for the ten-hour-plus flight via Singapore to Guam. Laura didn't sleep much on the plane. Mike and Marcus hit it off and chatted extensively. They arrived in Guam late, and would overnight there before taking the cargo plane over to Levati the following day. She shared a room with Lisa, the producer, while Marc bunked in with the cameraman and sound recordist. Mike Martin's status afforded him his own private room.

The closer they got to Levati, the more anxious she became. She had a disturbed sleep. Laura apologised to her roommate the following morning for tossing and turning all night, but the other woman was gracious. At least the nightmare hadn't embarrassed her. She felt tired and strained.

The crew started to film from the moment they arrived at the airport. There was film of them waiting, film of them boarding, film of them inside the plane. Laura felt very self-conscious, and had to try to stop and think before she did anything, in case it was recorded. Finally, there was a break from filming.

The flight on the cargo plane was four hours. Once land was

sighted, the cameraman started filming again. In the confined space, there was nowhere for her to hide. If she could've crawled under the seat, she would have. Mike Martin was asking Marcus a never-ending stream of questions about Levati, its issues, how he was feeling. Thankfully she was out of range, but she knew the camera was trained on her as she leant up against the plane window, willing the operator to look elsewhere for his shot. She kept still and eventually he got the hint, and put the camera away until they landed.

THERE WAS a lot of gear to lug to the waiting vehicles. Three Land Rovers were needed this trip. The drivers were less than impressed with requests to stop and start so the cameraman could film from different angles. It must've taken an extra hour to get to the hospital. The film crew went ahead so Marc and Laura's car could be filmed entering the compound. Once the luggage was dropped off, the crew followed Marc as he led the way into the building, so they could see where they would be filming. Introductions were made. Marcus knew the senior doctor on duty, but most of the other short-termers were new.

After scoping out the hospital and its surrounds, they sat down to plan what they wanted to film and formulated a run sheet. It was Marc's passion, so he was to be the main focus. Laura tried to be as inconspicuous as possible.

Before long, the two of them were seated with Mike around a staffroom table, talking. Well, Mike and Marcus were talking.

The cameraman was circling the table. Laura wasn't enjoying the interview process at all. It seemed they asked variations of the same questions at least five times. Marc wasn't fazed and varied his answers at least five times.

Laura could feel a hot lava flow of anger fighting its way to the surface. She struggled to hold it back, but couldn't. She snapped! Slamming her fist onto the table she exploded from her chair, knocking it over in the process, directing her anger at the cameraman.

"Damn, don't you ever turn that bloody thing off?"

Banging herself painfully on the corner of the table, she couldn't get out of the room fast enough, rushing to slam the door open and get out of camera range as fast as possible.

EVERYONE in the room was taken aback. The camera stopped rolling.

Marcus apologised. "Sorry, obviously, this has been harder on Laura than I thought." He went to follow her out the door. "I'll have a talk to her."

As he walked in the direction she had taken, Marcus was kicking himself for not keeping a closer eye on her. He should've seen it coming. Although he'd lost sight of her, he had an idea where she might be. There was a spot up behind the accommodation block—it would be out of sight of the staff area. He was right. She was sitting on a bench behind a tree, turning away when he sat next to her and waited.

"I can't do this, Marcus, it's too hard."

"Yes, you can, you'll get through it."

"Not with my every move being recorded. It's too much to handle."

"I know it's not easy, but I think it'll be beneficial in the long run."

"I'm scared, Marc. I don't want to go any further."

"You have to confront it, Laura. It will help you get closure so you can move on. You won't be on your own, remember. We will have an armed escort."

"I don't want to be on national television."

"Look, maybe we can come to some compromise with the crew so you can get some privacy to deal with the situation."

"Yeah sure. The bigger the meltdown the better the ratings."

"Stay here," he sighed. "I'll be back as soon as I can."

~

TEN MINUTES LATER HE RETURNED, with an assurance from Mike Martin and the others that they would agree to stop filming if she was too distressed. And then he had to work hard to convince her to go back, especially when she realised the cameras would be on them.

"We'll just wander a bit and give them some footage okay?" It seemed she wasn't about to move. "Look, they'll do the shots from a distance instead of in our faces, so it won't be so bad."

He held a hand out to her. Finally, she relented. He put his arm around her shoulder to steer her in the direction he had in mind. Glancing up, he saw where the cameraman was situated and turned so she was tucked up alongside his own body.

~

To LAURA it felt awkward and stilted as it had before, forcing herself to follow his lead. Gradually, though, she felt herself relax. Being alongside Marc did that sometimes. He showed enough affection but wasn't overly familiar.

Mike Martin did a piece to camera and then the focus turned to them. There was a walk around the compound with Mike. Marcus did the talking while keeping a firm, reassuring grip on her hand. Then, the mock ward visit, the coffee in the staffroom shot, the staff meeting shot, and on it went. Trying to keep the disruption to the hospital to a minimum was a balancing act.

The following day was the visit to the village. At first, the inhabitants were wary of the crew, but eventually they were won over enough to be filmed going about their daily lives. Finally, another day down, but tomorrow would be bigger. The US

Army were sending a helicopter to take them back to the base and then escort them to the remote clinic.

Laura hadn't expected to travel in a military chopper again. She remembered very little of the first trip. It had been a bit of a daze. She had been numb. Relieved to be getting away.

To some extent she enjoyed this flight, but every minute brought them closer to "that place". The commanding officer at the base hosted a dinner in their honour that night. Marc, as usual, looked right at ease, laughing and joking with the army personnel along with Mike Martin and the rest of the television crew.

As soon as was possible, Laura left them. They would be talking, no doubt, until the early hours. Slept evaded her, and when she eventually dozed off there were nightmares.

WHEN THE TIME came for them to head out to the clinic, nothing was left to chance. The four-vehicle convoy looked intimidating, like something you'd see on the news from conflict areas of the Middle East, but it didn't help Laura feel any more at ease.

They went the so-called "back way" which meant two hours of driving from the base and didn't follow the track Marc had used originally. The building was pretty much as they'd left it. There had been no clinics held since, and it was uncertain if there would be again. Negotiations were underway for the Americans to provide personnel to visit the area with the appropriate backup. As usual, Laura let Marcus do most of the talking.

Then they wanted to film down "the track". Laura baulked at the idea.

"We're not going very far, just to get something that looks like isolated track shots."

She wasn't reassured.

One of the army vehicles went ahead on the track and

waited, guns at the ready. The vehicle behind them was also on guard while the cameraman filmed from the second vehicle as Marc drove along the track. Dry-mouthed, Laura took one deep breath after another as she scanned the bush either side of the track, convinced someone would jump out at them at any moment. Logically she knew it would probably not happen, but she wasn't being very logical at present. On edge the whole time, she jumped at the slightest thing.

MARC WAS KEEPING a close eye on her, ready to call it all off in an instant if he thought it was getting too much. They had a pre-arranged signal to halt proceedings if he felt she wasn't coping. He came close a couple of times, when the strain seemed to swamp her. But they managed to get through the filming and get back to the base just on sunset. The night shots the crew wanted were filmed just outside the base perimeter. He breathed a sigh of relief when they finally decided they had enough film.

The helicopter flew them back to Guam. Mike Martin must've had some pull with the US Army. It was after midnight by the time they arrived back, totally exhausted from the trip.

CHAPTER TWENTY

rriving in Cairns, it was back to business. Marcus shook his head as he sorted through all the requests for speaking engagements. Laura sat opposite at his study desk, while he frowned and sighed.

"Marcus, there's a limit to what we can take on. We'll just have to turn some requests down."

"I don't like to," he replied, sifting through the pile for the umpteenth time. "Unless we..." He trailed off.

"Unless we what?"

He paused, unsure of the reaction he would get. He couldn't see her going for it, but he would just have to convince her otherwise. "Unless we split up for a while. We could cover more ground, fulfil more requests."

"But they'll want to see both of us, surely?"

"We'll just have to contact people and tell them it's one of us or nothing. We'll still do as many together as we can." There was silence from the other side of the table. He couldn't tell what was going on in her head.

LAURA DIDN'T KNOW what to make of the idea. She could see the sense in what he was proposing and, surely, she had done enough functions and other speaking engagements to go solo now.

And she really needed to put some distance between them anyway. He was too distracting. She couldn't count the number of times she'd lost her train of thought when she was speaking lately, because of the way he had looked at her or some little physical gesture he made that sent the heat curling through her body and triggered a wanton need to kiss him on the spot.

Maybe distance would help her calm down a little. She blew a breath out.

"If you think it will be for the best."

HMMM. He hadn't expected that. Why did she agree so willingly? Maybe she needed to be away from him for a while. He certainly didn't want to be away from her, but he wasn't about to tell her that. Instead he stuffed the thought down, out of reach.

It took a while and nearly did his head in, but he finally organised two separate itineraries.

"Maybe you need to think about getting someone else on board, temporarily, who can deal with the requests," she suggested tentatively.

He shook his head. "At this stage, I'd rather not, but it's something I'd be prepared to consider if it gets any more hectic. Okay then, we have that photo shoot next week and then from there we can go our own way. I'll make sure we've each got a copy of both itineraries, hotel lists, phone numbers and so on."

SHE SCANNED the handwritten sheet in front of her. "So, basically, we won't cross paths until the fundraising ball in Melbourne?"

"Doesn't look like it at this stage. Is it a problem?"

Yeah, it's a huge problem, she wanted to yell. *Don't leave me to do this on my own. I need your support to get through this. It's the only reason I've been able to, so far.* "No, not that I can see."

"Good, then I can get this lot typed up and we can get going." He'd hoped she'd refuse to go it alone. He had no doubt she was more than capable of managing. If the truth be told, he didn't want them to go their separate ways.

But, in the end, his commitment to the cause of Medi-Aid won over, reminding him it was ultimately about the money they could raise. That had to take precedence over his personal feeling for the woman he was supposedly engaged to.

WERE real-life fashion photo shoots really anything like what you see in the media? Laura was about to find out as they drove to a nondescript industrial estate in the backblocks of outer Sydney. A small sign alongside a solid metal door indicated they were at the right address. A young woman in tight black jeans and a little matching leather jacket over a white t-shirt came over, holding a clipboard, as they ventured inside. Her bright blue hair was pulled back into a severe ponytail, and she sported several ear piercings. Swapping the clipboard to her left hand, she reached out with her right to shake.

"Hi, I'm Samara. Marcus and Laura, right? I see you found the place okay." She led them through the building. The huge warehouse was buzzing with activity everywhere they looked.

"Sorry, it's a bit crazy here. It always is, though. We are in the middle of shooting an ad campaign, so we are working you guys in around that." The followed her in and out of what looked like different scenes set up in various "rooms".

She stopped and introduced them to another woman, Connie, who would be taking care of them. Laura thought Connie was about her own age. Shorter, but a real dynamo. Dressed in a businesslike black trouser suit and cream shirt, her red hair twisted up into a knot high on the top of her head and tied with a green ribbon, the same shade as her eyes. The silk scarf hanging around her neck was a swirl of greens and yellows. She wore black framed glasses and was writing on her own clipboard as she checked them out.

A couple of high profile Medi-Aid supporters had come up with the idea of a fundraising ball, and Marcus had let them run with it, forming a gala committee to oversee the night. The photo shoot was basically a promotional piece for the ball. The idea was to dress them in outfits by various designers as a fashion feature in an upcoming edition of *The Australian Women's Journal.*

Connie sent Laura in one direction and Marcus in another to get ready. The fashion editor had chosen a red dress for the first outfit. Laura let the hairstylist get to work and then the make-up artist. Marcus was already under lights by the time she was led out to join him. They didn't talk while the crew fussed around, adjusting lights and whatever else needed to be done. Marcus was wearing a black suit with a crimson vest and cummerbund to match her dress.

Laura found it awkward at first, following directions—where to stand and how to move. The initial concept was to get the idea of movement, so the fullness of the dress she was wearing could be displayed for the camera. The tight bodice was strapless with gold trim, and a long chiffon scarf completed the look. Marcus twirled and spun her according to what he was told, while Laura held out the skirt at every opportunity.

Relieved to be able to sit down for a few minutes, she waited for her hair to be redone to compliment the next dress. The short emerald green dress was unusual to say the least, with a detachable train that swept the floor, a bustle of some sort at the back and a huge bow. The ruched bodice had a square neckline and wide straps. Her hair had been pinned up at the sides with matching emerald combs. A black and emerald necklace and earrings were added. The outfit was completed with long silk gloves and fishnet stockings.

You have got to be kidding me! Laura shook her head at her reflection in the mirror. It was something akin to what would be worn by women in a saloon in a movie about the Wild West.

Marcus greeted her with a raised eyebrow.

"Don't you dare say anything," she warned under her breath.

He simply held his hands up and backed away with a slight teasing grin.

Once the photographer set to work, the "green jokes" came flying thick and fast from all directions. It seemed everyone in the building had gravitated towards their spot. Laura decided to take it all in good humour. Before long they were all laughing at the corny lines as they attempted to outdo each other.

"You lot are making me sick," she told them, tongue in cheek.

"You certainly look green around the gills," one of the lighting fellows shot back.

"Ha ha," she retorted dryly.

Marcus started singing, "It's not easy being green," just loud enough for Laura to hear.

She held her peace until the photographer gave the all clear and then she whacked him on the chest.

"Alright you, that's enough." She stalked off in mock anger to change again.

A long time later, Laura surveyed the last in a seemingly endless line of outfits in the mirror. In reality, it was probably only half a dozen, none of which had appealed to her.

"Now, this is better," she said to herself. The soft black folds of the cowl neckline fell gracefully from the thin straps. The dress hugged her figure as it skimmed the floor with a thigh high split and an alarmingly low back.

She would never have thought she could pull off this look. But she had to admit she felt very sexy, turning to gain the full effect in front of the full-length mirror as it reflected her image from the mirrors behind and to the side. Pearl drop earrings with a matching necklace and bracelet completed the ensemble. Audrey Hepburn, eat your heart out. The hair stylist pulled a stray wisp of hair into place and proclaimed Laura ready.

Marcus was sitting on a stool, engrossed in conversation with one of the technicians, when she walked out of the dressing room. Dressed in a superbly cut white suit, his back was turned slightly towards her, so he was oblivious to her approach.

The photographer came over quietly to her side. "I want to try something different. When I give you the signal, I want you to walk over to where Marc is sitting and attract his attention. He hasn't realised you are about, and I want to try and capture his natural reaction to seeing you in that."

Laura did as she was asked. Once the photographer was ready, he signalled to Laura who walked over to Marcus. The room fell silent. She got to within a couple of metres before he noticed the lack of noise and looked up, turning to follow everyone's gaze. The look of stunned disbelief was priceless, as his gaze swept slowly up and down her figure while she waited.

Recovering quickly, he stood up, aware that the camera was clicking. Taking her arm, he led her to the spot where they were to stand, all the while not taking his eyes off her face. Laura was captivated by the intense look of—what was it? desire?—in his eyes.

The atmosphere was highly charged. She could practically hear the air crackle as time stood still. His blue eyes were penetrating deep into her very soul and Laura was sure he could see exactly how she felt. She wet her lips. It seemed like he was about to lean forward.

Someone in the crew wolf whistled and Laura looked away, breaking the spell. The general studio noise began again as Laura and Marcus moved as they were told.

This series of photos were to be different to the others, more intimate and sensual. It was easy for Laura to play the part; she didn't have to try too hard to enjoy the close physical contact. The white suit on her partner looked devastating, contrasting with her own black dress. Before long, the photographer had her standing, to take full advantage of the thigh-high split. Marcus stood behind her, one hand around her waist and the other stretching her arm out, kissing her shoulder as directed. Then he pulled her in close for a slow dance pose. His strong, firm fingers burning an indelible mark on her bare back. The heat he generated in her from that close proximity convinced her that she was on the point of spontaneous combustion. She hoped there was a fire extinguisher handy.

Once the photographer was satisfied he had all the shots he needed, they wrapped it up. Seemingly reluctant to let her go, Marcus held her for longer than was necessary. Laura eased herself gently out of his arms, when she really wanted to stay right where she was. He'd hardly said a word the whole time, although if she could believe what his eyes and arms were telling her, the message was loud and clear. He wanted her as much as she desired him.

Back in her street clothes, Laura was pleased she had chosen a comfortable pair of pants and a baggy pink sweatshirt. It was about as far away from the glamorous outfit she had just worn as she could get. Carefully, she removed all traces of makeup before she left the studio.

Marcus was wearing jeans and a brown leather jacket over a navy shirt, but to Laura he looked as devastating as he had a few minutes ago. He looked good in whatever he wore.

They caught a taxi back to the Sydney CBD and stopped for a bite to eat at a small café. Marcus was unnaturally quiet, and Laura allowed him to be preoccupied, content to mull over the photographic session herself.

Back at the hotel, she only saw him again just before he was due to leave for the airport. A few quick words about the schedule over the coming weeks and he was gone.

AN OVERWHELMING FEELING of emptiness threatened to engulf Laura as she tried to juggle her solo itinerary and keep up with the heavy round of engagements. She didn't expect to hear from Marcus often. He had been busy on a trip to the UK, followed closely by a three-week stint in the States. The world had been beating a path to their door to learn first-hand about the "Kidnap Couple". Messages from Marcus were often waiting for her at the hotel desks wherever she happened to be staying. Likewise, she dutifully reported every few days on her own experiences.

Late one night in Adelaide, she was roused from sleep by the phone. Groping around in the unfamiliar room for the handset she was startled to hear his voice.

"Laura?"

"Mmmm."

"It's Marc. Sorry, sweetheart, I didn't mean to wake you." She struggled upright, assuring him it was okay.

"I just needed to hear your voice." Laura sank back into the pillows, a warm glow filling her as she took in his words. "Laura, are you still there?"

"Yes, sorry, I'm still waking up… How's things going?" she asked, hoping he would give her enough time to pull herself together. After a few minutes, she launched into a commentary of her last few days. To be honest, she prattled on a bit just to keep him on the phone a little longer, pleased to hear his voice as well. He suddenly stopped her mid-sentence.

"If I listen to you much more, I'll ditch the program here and get the next available flight home."

"Homesick, huh?"

"No…" She heard him blow out a breath. "Just got used to having you around. I guess I kind of miss you a bit."

Laura missed him a bit as well, wishing she could teleport herself to New York to visit. It was going to be a long few weeks.

MARC PLACED the phone back in its cradle, and stared out at the New York skyline, thinking about the long day ahead. Hearing her wasn't enough. He longed to see her. More than that he wanted to hold her in his arms again and breathe in the scent of her.

All he could do was count down the days until he could get back to her.

CHAPTER TWENTY-ONE

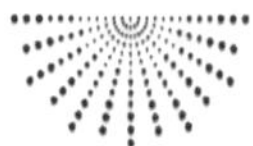

The promotional feature for the fundraising ball came out in *The Australian Women's Journal* two weeks before the gala. All it could do was raise awareness and hopefully garner some more donations, because tickets for the ball had been snapped up within a couple of hours of being released.

Laura had gone to the designer of the "black dress" for her ball outfit. It was a stunning royal blue number, and Laura was thrilled with the end result. The final fitting included the accessories she was to wear to complement the dress. The style was more than reminiscent of the gorgeous dark blue silk-velvet number the Princess of Wales had worn to the White House when she famously danced with John Travolta.

Laura felt and looked like a princess. Surprisingly, she was actually looking forward to the ball.

Just before she was due to speak at a businesswomen's conference in Brisbane, she received a call from Sydney airport.

"Well, I'm back in the country… exhausted, but back."

Laura could hear the bone weariness in his voice. "Great, but don't push it. Go and grab some sleep—otherwise you won't be much good."

"Laura, I'll always be good for you." Was she was reading way too much into those words?

She insisted. "Still, I'd feel better if you were over your jet lag."

"Okay Mum, I'll take things easy and see you in a couple of days."

He didn't see her in a couple of days. He was struck down with the flu. Laura insisted he stay where he was and rest. He was too sick to argue. She phoned him at least twice a day to check on him, but he consistently refused her entreaties to fly to Sydney and nurse him.

Once he was back on deck, some of the talk shows snaffled him for interviews, so she wouldn't get to see him until the night of the ball.

"I'll be there, no matter what," he promised, as a snap pilots' strike grounded all flights out of Sydney.

Laura surveyed her reflection in the full-length mirror in her Melbourne hotel suite. The material draped around her body on an angle which revealed her shapely figure. The pearl and sapphire necklace had been adjusted so it sat at the perfect length, just above the sweetheart curve of the neckline. With the matching earrings and bracelet, she hated to think how much the borrowed jewels cost, grateful the designer had entrusted them to her to wear. She hoped she'd be able to do justice to the designer's outfit, knowing that the public interest in what she wore could be hugely beneficial to the company.

The hairstylist had swept her hair up with a couple of loose tendrils either side of her face. If she were a member of the Royal Family, she guessed a tiara would have been the finishing touch.

She walked back and forth a few times to make sure she could handle the heels she was wearing.

Time was getting away. If Marcus didn't arrive soon, they would be late to their own function. The knock on the door sent her quickly to greet him. She smoothed a nervous hand down her dress, then answered the door. If Laura thought she had wowed him with that black dress at the photo shoot, she completely floored him tonight.

His first words confirmed it. "I didn't think you could look any better than you did in that black number but, obviously, I was wrong. Hi, Laura, you look sensational." He leaned down and kissed her briefly.

She studied his features with concern. "You look tired, Marcus." She reached for her clutch and wrap before closing the door behind her.

"Yeah, well I had quite a roundabout way to get here." He told her of his trip while they walked to the elevator. His thoughts were scattering everywhere, such was the effect she was having on him. She was stunning. That dress, her hair and makeup and, oh, that perfume! The tantalising scent of her was making him lightheaded. He had to fight the desire to stop and pull her into his arms and never let her go. Daring to put a hand on the small of her back was tantamount to losing control, and he was expected to make a speech tonight. Heaven help him—he could barely string coherent sentences together.

"Oh, Marcus, you should have stayed put," she exclaimed, after hearing how he'd driven two hours to charter a plane, only to have it divert due to a severe storm.

He kissed the hand he was holding. "It was worth it, believe me. If only I didn't have to fly on to Perth."

"When will the pilots' strike be finished?"

"At midnight. I've been able to get on an early flight… But enough of that, let's just go and enjoy ourselves for a few hours."

A BLACK LIMOUSINE had been sent for them, even though it was just a short drive to the gala venue. As they alighted from the vehicle there was even red carpet waiting, along with a crush of paparazzi and fans. Marcus stepped out ahead and waited for Laura to join him. Her grip on his hand tightened as she realised the extent of the crowd lined up either side of the roped off area.

"Oh my!" she whispered. "This is too much." She took a slight backward step before he stopped her.

"Relax, it will be okay, you will be fine." His hand moved to her elbow as he guided her along the red pathway laid out in front of the building. There was even a backdrop with the Medi-Aid logo and those of the evening's sponsors, where the guests were pausing to have their photographs taken.

The actual walk to the main entrance wasn't a long one, but to Laura it was like something she had only ever seen on television, at a movie premiere or awards ceremony. Marcus moved Laura closer to his side as voices came at them from every angle —and those flashes.

How did celebrities cope with all of this, Laura wondered, her smile stuck in place. She knew that among the crowd gathered inside tonight would be a veritable who's who of Australian society, from politicians to entertainers, sporting personalities to captains of industry. It was incredible to think a function of this magnitude could be pulled together in such a short time frame with such an impressive guest list.

LAURA PAUSED at the top of the grand staircase that led to the foyer of the beautiful Plaza Ballroom. As nervous as she felt, she still managed to take in the splendour of the restored building. It was comparable to a grand nineteenth century European ballroom. The detail of the Spanish-style courtyard was almost invisible under the milling throng of people, except, of course, for the ornate fountain in the centre.

Laura made sure she had a firm grip on Marc's arm as they descended the staircase to where the pre-dinner drinks were being served. The flutter of nerves intensified as she was introduced to various guests. Marcus took the lead, talking to the people around them. Laura pressed closer to his side as the mass of people around them grew in size. Everyone, it seemed, was keen for a chat. Marcus took it all in his stride and Laura envied his confident manner. No one would know he was so tired. Game face was on.

Finally, Laura breathed a sigh of relief as they were escorted to their table, resplendent with crisp white tablecloth and gleaming cutlery alongside the white-on-white crockery. Tables had been arranged in long lengths radiating out from the centre of the room. Tall centrepieces at regular intervals sparkled like falling fireworks alongside the smaller, round, frosted tea light holders. Marc's hand on her lower back gently guided her to their seats. He pulled her chair back and waited until she settled before sitting down alongside.

Laura tried to take in her surroundings discreetly, not knowing where to look first. The intricacy of the Spanish Rococo architecture was mesmerising. She learned the high ceilings and custom-made chandeliers were original from 1929. Juliet balconies ringed the room and she wouldn't mind betting the leather chairs were Italian—probably handmade at that.

The food was impressive, served in an alternate drop. After the entrée, Marcus enjoyed spice-crusted beef tenderloin and a dark chocolate mousse for dessert. Laura's main was a slow roasted lamb loin followed by a dessert of orange pannacotta. It was delicious, but Laura was too keyed up to eat much.

It was nerve-racking to say the least, with the prime minister and his wife to one side of them and the state premier and his partner on the other. Around her, Laura recognised most of the high-flying guests from the media, who had paid top dollar to be seated at the head table. It was a humbling experience.

Marcus, as usual, seemed unfazed, joking with the Australian leader as they ate and helping himself to Laura's leftovers.

Between courses there were speeches; the last one was from Marcus. Laura was grateful that he was going to speak on behalf of them both this evening. She didn't like the idea of appearing on the large screen behind the dais. In all honesty, Laura didn't pay much attention to Marc's speech; in fact she zoned out because she had heard it all many times before.

But something caught her attention and she quickly tuned in.

~

"I KNOW you'll excuse me if I seem a little distracted tonight. Having spent three tough weeks in captivity with Laura, it's hard to believe it's the same person sitting next to me. It's quite a stunning transformation… not that she doesn't look good in whatever she wears." He paused a moment before continuing. "I'm going to finish by doing something totally unplanned."

Marcus hesitated before he plunged ahead. He could see Laura looking over at him, puzzled. He was taking a huge risk in public he knew, but he hoped it would pay off.

"As you know from all the media reports, part of the ruse we used to gain our freedom was to pretend we were married, and Laura is still wearing my signet ring I gave her to that end. Although I know she would never give it up, it's a poor substitute for the real thing… so, ladies and gentlemen, with your permission, I'd like to present my fiancée with this ring."

With that, he pulled a small black velvet box from his jacket pocket, which appeared on the big screen as the camera man zoomed in. Taking the couple of steps towards her, he reached out and waited until she accepted his hand and rose to join him at the podium. Applause surrounded them as Laura fumbled to swap the signet ring to her other hand. Marcus flipped the box open to reveal the most beautiful sapphire and diamond engagement ring. He pushed it onto her finger. A perfect fit. As the applause died down, he made a spur of the moment decision.

"I haven't seen Laura for a few weeks and just flew in tonight in time for this function. So, if you'll excuse me, there's something I've been wanting to do all evening."

With that, he turned his back on the audience and drew the unsuspecting Laura into his arms and kissed her soundly. He just about brought the house down.

Lifting his head, he grinned slowly at her stunned features. Turning back to the microphone, he announced it was time to start dancing. Without giving Laura time to protest he led her out onto the floor. After a few minutes alone in the spotlight, they were joined by others.

Marcus pulled back slightly to look at her. "Well?" he asked.

"Well what?" she murmured, still clearly taken aback by the last few minutes.

"You seem to be at a loss for words." Laura barely nodded as he chuckled and pulled her in against him as they moved to the music.

LAURA WAS SPEECHLESS, never anticipating Marcus would make such a public admission. She closed her eyes and enjoyed the feeling of being in his arms as they circled the floor. The warmth and strength as he led her in a firm but gentle grip. Accustomed to dancing with him now, as they had done many times at various functions, she easily matched her steps with his.

However, tonight was different somehow, and it wasn't just because of the ring. There was another level of connection that she had never noticed before. She very much liked the feel of whatever this was between them, as he leaned towards her for a quick kiss.

~

IT WASN'T long before the prime minister cut in and Laura was swept away from her fiancé. Marcus was polite and charming to his partners, but his gaze kept following her around the room. She looked stunning from any angle tonight. Confident, sexy, and laughing with each man, doing exactly what she was supposed to be doing. Charming them. The butterfly had well and truly emerged.

He remembered the first awkward couple of times they had danced together until they learned each other's nuances. He couldn't help feeling jealous of each man who got to dance with her. They were where he desperately wanted to be, holding her close and breathing in that heavenly scent she was wearing tonight. Heck, he was even jealous of the leader of the country for daring to cut in.

~

LAURA CHANGED PARTNERS REGULARLY, and didn't catch more than a glimpse of Marcus from time to time. She answered the idle chatter of her partners as best she could, but was always scanning the crowd hoping to see his familiar figure. It wasn't until the early hours that they found each other… just when it was time to leave.

Surprisingly, the vast foyer was almost empty as they made their way through. Seizing the opportunity, Marcus steered her into one of the alcoves that lined the walls. Almost hidden from view, she went willingly into his arms as his mouth claimed her eager lips.

Hungrily, she returned his kisses, pressing herself closer to his athletic frame. His tongue found its way to join with hers.

Her wrap slipped to the floor unheeded as she lost herself in the fervour of his embrace. Laura's hands slipped inside his jacket and she delighted in running her hands around his waist and up over the hard strength of his chest. He groaned her name as he rained kisses over her face, her neck, her bare shoulders. She shivered at every delicious sensation that was enveloping her and clung to him as desire exploded deep within her and threatened to consume her.

WITH GREAT DIFFICULTY, Marcus called a halt, stroking her face gently. He apologised. "I should never have started something that I can't finish."

Laura found herself reaching for his hand, kissing the palm tenderly. He tilted her head so he could look deep into her brown eyes.

"Will you hold that thought until I get back?"

Laura closed her eyes and swallowed. Would she wait until he got back to...? She nodded slowly.

He kissed her gently before bending to retrieve her wrap. Enclosing her in its luxurious folds, he walked her out and signalled to the waiting limousine. Marcus took one last lingering look at the beautiful woman beside him before seeing her into the car. "I'll be with you soon," he promised. He tapped on the roof of the limo and the driver pulled away from the kerb.

LAURA EXISTED IN A DREAMLIKE STATE. She barely remembered getting out of the limousine and returning to her hotel room. For once, the night terrors eluded her and she slept late.

Her sense of warmth and general well-being was cruelly shattered by the late edition of the morning paper. There it was, not on the front—page seven to be exact—but significant none the less.

"Doctor Marcus Bradley, recently held captive on the island of Levati, caused quite a stir among the guests at the Medi-Aid fundraising ball last night when he presented his unsuspecting fiancée, Laura Maxwell, with a sapphire and diamond engagement ring at the conclusion of his speech."

As Laura continued to read, in the harsh light of day she saw last night for what it really was: another publicity stunt. She should have known.

Cursing herself for being so gullible, Laura flung the paper across the room, scattering its pages on the floor. Angrily she went to have a shower, but she could still feel his touch on her body. Turning the heat and pressure up higher did not go any way towards erasing the feelings he had evoked in her last night.

To incite her under false pretences, all to increase the publicity stakes, was contemptible. Catching sight of the twin stones of the sapphire and diamond ring on her finger, Laura burst into tears, remaining under the shower for as long as the emotional deluge continued.

Stepping over the morning's news and gossip columns, Laura calmly cancelled the next couple of days' speaking engagements. Pulling her hair up under a cap and wearing dark sunglasses, she escaped into the city streets, indistinguishable from the other casually dressed people out and about. Clad in jeans and an old sweatshirt, she went where she pleased and did what she wanted, unrestricted by timetables, speaking schedules and media appearances. Jumping on a tram, she headed for the port, almost tempted to board the Tasmania-bound ferry docked nearby. Instead she wandered along the foreshore, head down, trying to avoid drawing attention to herself.

～

IT WAS late before she got back to her hotel room. She'd hardly set her bag down when the phone rang. Laura knew it would be Marcus and debated whether to answer—but knew she would have to deal with him eventually, and it may as well be now.

"Where have you been?" he demanded as soon as she picked up the receiver.

"Out," she answered coolly.

"You cancelled speaking engagements. Why?"

"I decided I needed a break."

"I wish you'd consulted me first."

"Why? Upsets the precious publicity apple cart, does it?"

"You're in a foul mood this evening. Annoyed because we didn't follow through last night?"

"Hardly," she retorted.

"Have you seen the newspapers?" he asked.

"Boy, you've certainly outdone yourself this time, Marc. Is there nothing you won't stoop to in order to gain a little more publicity?"

"Pardon?"

"How long did it take you to come up with that little stunt? I must admit it was pretty good. You not only convinced the guests at the ball, you had me fooled as well."

"You seriously think it was all a stunt?" he asked.

"It could hardly be anything else. What a good ploy. You knew I wouldn't do anything in front of all those people. A captive audience to see the hero doctor confirm his commitment to his fiancée. You make me sick."

"Laura, I—"

She cut him off angrily. "Surely you're not going to try and tell me it wasn't all for the papers?"

"You obviously wouldn't believe me if I told you any different."

"No."

"Well, I guess there is nothing more to say. I'll see you in two days."

Laura slammed the phone down quickly, her eyes smarting from unshed tears, but she refused to give way again. She would not cry any more tears over Marcus Bradley.

When two days turned into two weeks, Laura didn't mind in the least. Of course, the engagement ring was a new source of interest. She answered questions about the event if asked, but otherwise it was business as usual. The longer Marcus was away, the stronger she felt.

CHAPTER TWENTY-TWO

*D*espite schooling herself, her heart did an involuntary flip as soon as Marcus walked into the small meeting room at her hotel. She dropped her gaze. Damn, she still hadn't been able to shake off the effect he had on her.

Responding coolly to his greeting, she shuffled the pile of letters, faxes and other papers, waiting for him to get a cup of coffee and join her at the table to discuss the latest round of requests for interviews and appearances. Trying not to let his demeanour put her off the task at hand, she reeled off the information quickly from the highlighted portions she had already marked on each page. As she spoke, Marcus took notes.

"The committee organising Volunteers' Week are looking for a spokesman and were wondering if either of us were interested. There's an overseas aid workers' conference in five months in Prague, and they are hoping you'll be the keynote speaker. We have three school fete invitations, one in Queensland and two in New South Wales. There's also a couple of requests to open country shows. *The Australian Women's Journal* is keen to know if we have set a wedding date and want to offer a deal for exclusive photos. Your father's sent a message to remind you that you promised to attend the Australasian Surgeons' Symposium in

Cairns in October and there are half a dozen requests for personal items to be donated for charity auctions."

"I think we should…" he trailed off.

"Should what?" she queried.

"Set a wedding date."

"You've got to be crazy! No more stunts, Marcus, no way!"

"What is the magazine prepared to offer?"

Laura pushed the pile of papers across the table with barely concealed disgust. Jumping up, she paced the room as he calmly sorted through the papers and found the sheet he was looking for.

He was quiet for a minute then let out a long whistle. "It's a lot of money, Laura."

"No, Marcus, I won't."

"You promised to play the part."

"In terms of speaking engagements and interviews, but not this."

"It'll be no different from pretending to be engaged…"

"Garbage, Marcus! It's a legal contract we'd be entering into. How could you possibly expect me to stand at an altar some-where and make vows that are hollow and empty and don't mean a thing?"

"I'm sure plenty of other couples have married for convenience."

"Yeah, in a romance novel maybe, not real life. When I get married, I want it to be for all the right reasons, not because I could stand to earn a lot of money for my favourite charity."

"It's the last so-called stunt I'll ask you to do."

"And I suppose the divorce comes as part of the package."

"Of course, if that's what want."

"I don't want anything, except my life back, Marcus. I've had about as much as I can stand of this whole charade."

～

Marcus made no response, instead he reached for the phone nearby and began to punch in some numbers.

"What are you up to?" she demanded.

"You want out? Fine. But you won't be able to do anything without a blaze of publicity. I'm going to the press for an exclusive on the breakdown of our relationship."

"You wouldn't!" Laura dived for the phone, but he swept her away.

"Whichever way this goes, Laura, I intend to milk it for all it's worth. You need to understand I will do whatever I have to in order to promote Medi-Aid. And if that means a 'tell all' to the media, then so be it." He was calling her bluff. Her reaction made him uncomfortable but he chose to focus on the publicity it would generate either way.

What had he become? Was he really so caught up in promoting the cause that he would be prepared to enter a marriage of convenience? It would add a whole other dynamic to their relationship. Could they even pull it off? His doubts needed to be shoved out of the way, so he could plough on, regardless.

"You can choose to end it all now and cop the flak that will go with it, or we go through with the wedding and evoke public sympathy down the track when the marriage inevitably breaks down."

Laura sat down as if she had been physically winded. Where on earth had this come from? It didn't make any sense. Who was the man sitting across the table from her? Obviously, she didn't know him as well as she thought. Angela Reid's comments back on Levati about not getting in his way when it came to Medi-Aid came back to taunt her.

After she recovered from the initial shock, she guessed she could see some of his reasoning. But it was getting out of hand. Wasn't it? One minute she was aghast at the whole idea and the next she felt she was wavering. He launched into some compelling arguments to justify taking this course of action. Maybe she should approach it like a business arrangement. But there was too much emotion for it to just be a commercial transaction.

And how could he even contemplate entering into a marriage in name only? Didn't his conscience bother him as much as she was struggling with hers? Didn't he value the vows of marriage? From all his talk about his parents' marriage, she thought he did—but it didn't seem to bother him to throw his beliefs out the window. Maybe she was being too precious. Maybe it would be worthwhile. Maybe it would work out okay. People married and divorced all the time, right? Maybe she was old-fashioned to hold on to an idealistic view of marriage in this day and age. Look at her parents' marriage—it had never been great. And her father's second marriage… well…

The thoughts in her head struggled to gain a foothold. Tumbling around like a clothes dryer. Tossed together. It was a tough decision.

"Sorry, what did you say?" she said.

"We need to make a decision."

Her answer was supposed to be no—but that's not what came out of her mouth. Even Marcus seemed surprised when she said yes.

CHAPTER TWENTY-THREE

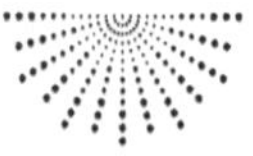

*A*fter consulting his diary, Marcus announced a date in six weeks' time.

"I actually don't think I want to know the details. I'm not sure why I'm agreeing to this. If you want to do it so badly, then you can do the organising. I won't be involved in any of the planning. Just tell me the time and place and I'll be there." She rubbed at the goosebumps on her arms as he considered her request.

"Very well. I'll agree to that."

Marcus knew he had a tight deadline, but he also knew that if *The Australian Women's Journal* wanted the exclusive on the wedding, they would be all too willing to pull out all stops to assist in its organisation.

He received recommendations for several dress designers. Once that was sorted, everything else seemed to fall into place without too much drama. There were plenty of people keen to play a part in the happy event. The hotel he preferred managed to find space for a small reception. The church where his parents married had one time slot available for his chosen day.

He still had no real idea why he had pushed for the wedding. Yes, the money for Medi-Aid was good.

But…?

But what?

If he was really honest, he wanted to be married to Laura. Their whole relationship so far had been unconventional. It seemed to work. Well, he had convinced himself it worked. He knew she had feelings for him, at least as strong as he had for her.

She'd surprised him when she'd agreed to go along with the charade. In all honesty, he hadn't expected her to go for it. But once they were married, he would do all he could to help her see they were right for each other.

LAURA STOOD in front of the full-length mirror as Danielle Bradley finished fastening the dress. She couldn't believe she was actually going to go through with this. What was she thinking?

Because you'd do anything for Marcus Bradley, you little fool.

"There, that about does it," Danielle told her, straightening up to survey the effect. "You look incredible. This dress is so perfect for you. I don't know how Marcus pulled it off."

Danielle didn't know all the wedding backstory, though she knew Marc had worked tirelessly to get everything in place. What she didn't know was that Laura had had nothing to do with the prep.

Laura, shaking her head at her reflection in the mirror, wasn't about to enlighten her. She didn't know how he had managed to pull everything off in six weeks, either. This dress. Despite the fittings, she'd had no idea how the finished gown would look. Marc had chosen the designer well. Her upswept hair showcased the neckline, scalloped and edged with delicate embroidered navy flowers and leaves that formed a v shape down the top of the bodice. The edges of the capped sleeves were also embroidered. The material swept around her on an angle. The waist on the left-hand side featured more flowers and leaves that encircled her waist and travelled up the bodice. A navy panel peeked out from underneath the embroidered section, falling to the floor. The pearl earrings and necklace were a family heirloom, worn by Emma Bradley on her wedding day and by Danielle when she married Stephen.

Ashlee and Jacinta sat primly on a nearby couch, afraid to move and earn their mother's wrath. Their hair was piled high in ringlets. Laura recalled their squeals of delight at dinner the previous evening when Uncle Marc had presented them with the miniature pearl necklaces and earrings they now wore. They were adorable in long pink dresses, with full skirts that stopped just short of the floor, revealing matching pale pink ballet flats. The navy sashes around their waists matched the fabric of their mother's long dress. Danielle's figure was well suited to the soft flowing style with capped sleeves and a simple bateau neckline.

Her almost-sister-in-law came to her with a beautifully wrapped box.

"Marc asked me to give this to you about now."

The pale blue marbled paper was set off by a huge rich-blue bow. Laura took the box with nervous fingers, placed it on the table nearby, and opened it under Danielle's curious gaze.

Pushing aside the tissue paper, Laura lifted out an exquisite nightgown. Sheer white material trimmed with pale blue ribbon spilled out of the box. Her hand shook a little as she pulled out the card. *Looking forward to seeing you in this. M.*

She couldn't help but feel the flush of her cheeks.

"Laura, it's gorgeous. Do you want me to put it with your other things?"

"Ah, yes, I guess," Laura replied absently, determined to shove the gift out of her thoughts.

She took her place in front of the mirror and waited for Danielle to adjust the veil and headpiece.

~

THANKFULLY THERE WAS no photographer at the hotel with them. The car waiting downstairs was a two-toned blue 1951 Bentley with white wall tyres. She knew her father would be impressed when she arrived to meet him in it.

As the crow flies, the hotel wasn't far from the church, but there were several one-way streets to negotiate between the two. Laura knew Marcus had chosen the very same Brisbane church his parents had married in. She was uncomfortable with all the tradition and symbolism attached to the ceremony, but she realised Marc wanted to ensure it was a "real wedding". She felt such a fraud and hadn't wanted any friends and family to be there to witness the charade, but she'd had to provide some names to Marcus.

Everything took on a surreal atmosphere as she made her way to the one hundred and twenty-year-old red-brick church. The magazine photographer stepped over to her. Thankfully, there were no hordes of people waiting to see her arrive, as the wedding had been kept a secret. Her father was waiting at the top of the stairs. She took his arm, grateful for his support as the music started up. The twins took their cue and walked slowly down the aisle with well-practised steps.

Danielle put a hand on her shoulder briefly. "Are you okay?" she whispered.

Laura bit her lip and swallowed nervously, nodding her head.

"You'll be fine. Just focus on the man at the front who loves you and is waiting for you to join him." With that, Danielle was gone.

Laura didn't want to focus on Marcus. She wanted to bolt

from the church and run, and keep running, but she was trapped.

"C'mon, sweetheart, let's go."

She readied herself to make that long walk down the aisle with her father. All these people about to be deceived by this lie, this sham, all for the sake of some publicity. Nervous anger—yeah that was how she was feeling.

Laura was sure she was about to lose it, when Marcus came into view, waiting with Stephen and the minister.

~

MARCUS COULDN'T TAKE his eyes off Laura. The dress looked amazing on her. She looked gorgeous. The veil obscured her eyes, so he couldn't be sure if she was just plain nervous, or maybe angry with him for putting her in this position. Both, he guessed.

He watched as she walked down the aisle clutching her father's arm, half expecting her to become a runaway bride. Whatever happened, the publicity would be worth a mint.

He admonished himself—he couldn't believe it had come to this. He shouldn't have let it happen.

~

LAURA KNEW she couldn't run, even if she wanted to. His intense gaze made sure of it. Those piercing blue eyes were like magnets, drawing her in.

They were the only ones who knew the truth. Marcus was prepared to go through with it, so she had better be as well. She dropped her gaze as she reached the front of the church, unable to look at his eyes another second.

John Maxwell handed his daughter over and she was on her own.

Unable to find a voice to join the singing of the first hymn,

Laura listened as if from far away, the sounds muffled. She was lost in her own thoughts. This couldn't be happening; how could she be standing here in front of all these people, ready and willing to make a mockery of the sanctity of the vows of marriage? How could she have possibly gotten into this mess?

She closed her eyes to try and shut everything out. What could she do? What should she do? She didn't want to be here.

"Liar," a voice told her. *"You're here because you really want to be here."*

"Why?" she answered the inner voice.

"Because you love Marcus Bradley."

Her eyes flew open. *"Pardon?"*

"You heard me, Laura Catherine Maxwell. You love Doctor Bradley and if this is what it takes to be with him, then you'll do it."

She cast a glance sideways. The voice was in her head, but it was right.

Finally, she had the courage to admit to herself the real reason she was standing at the altar of this church. She loved Marcus Bradley and wanted to be his wife. Despite the circumstances, it was where she wanted to be. For how long, she had no idea. But it would be worth it to be his wife for however long he decided to continue the relationship. Laura knew she wouldn't be the one to end it; the longer it went on, the better.

That acknowledgment suddenly brought everything into sharp focus. Letting out a slow breath, she prepared to make her vows, confident she could follow through.

Laura repeated the words that suddenly meant something, in a clear tone without a hint of nerves or regret. Marcus continued as he took one of the gold bands from the Bible held out to him. He sounded sincere, but to Laura it no longer mattered if he was or not. The difference was, she was sincere. She watched as he slid the ring onto her finger and pushed it into place. Taking the other circle of gold without shaking, she spoke her lines. There was no tremor in her voice as she moved the ring into position.

Marcus lifted her veil. She looked up at him and held his

gaze without fear or embarrassment. He bent his head to deliver the traditional kiss, which she accepted and returned.

He locked eyes with her again. A slight flicker of surprise registered in the blueness, then it was gone.

The register was duly signed, then Doctor and Mrs Bradley were presented to the congregation. Laura took his arm as they made their way back down the aisle, stopping to receive congratulatory hugs from all sides. Word must have gotten out, as there was a small crowd outside the church. The front steps afforded those at street level a good view of the bride and groom and they were greeted with warm applause.

BEFORE THEY WERE USHERED to the reception, there were the obligatory photos. They were becoming used to the whole process. Sean Cullen, the photographer, they knew of course from the first magazine shoot. He quickly got to work, setting up the family photos first, then the wedding party. The grand hotel staircase was always a favoured backdrop for wedding photos and Sean also made use of it.

Then he got Ashlee and Jacinta on their own. They played beautifully to the camera. Laura stood back and watched as Marcus got down on his haunches with Ashlee on one side standing away a bit on his right and Jacinta on the other side reaching out with her hand on his shoulder. A delightful shot. As soon as Sean finished, they rushed their uncle and smothered him with kisses until he begged for mercy.

Laura imagined what he would be like with his own children, easily picturing him with girls like the twins. Just then he glanced up and she was caught out. Sending the girls off to harass someone else, he rose to his feet and came over to where she was leaning back on a wall.

"I'm curious to know what you were thinking about just then?" he quizzed.

She was honest. "I was just imagining you with your own girls one day. Two little blonde bombshells with the killer blue eyes just like their dad."

"That's funny. I was imagining you with two dark haired beauties and I was hoping they would have the same melting chocolate eyes, like their mother," he replied, tugging gently on a loose wisp of her hair, before lightly brushing her cheek.

Laura was busy studying the flowers in her bouquet, willing herself not to react to his touch, and failing.

"Laura." Marcus spoke quietly. "Something's happened. Your demeanour has changed. When you walked down the aisle, I could sense animosity bubbling under the surface, maybe a bit of fear mixed in there as well… but by the end of the first hymn everything had changed. You were more serene instead of hostile. Why?"

She hesitated, unsure what to say.

"Laura, please."

She decided to put it all out there, but she couldn't look at him while she did. "Maybe I just realised the antagonism was a waste of time… that I was kidding myself… maybe because I realised I was going through with all of this because I wanted to, not because I had to…"

She trailed off as he let out a deep, slow breath at her admission.

～

"ARE YOU SURE?"

She nodded slightly.

He wanted to say more. An apology was owing. He was sorry, but at the same time not. They were called by the photographer for more shots, so his words went unspoken for now.

With the night-time lights of the Brisbane River as a backdrop, he and Laura waited to be directed into position. Desperate to get her alone to find out more about her change of heart, he needed to look into her eyes and see it for himself. But he had to be patient. He wasn't doing so well in that regard.

THERE WAS one shot in particular Laura knew would be the shot of the day—well, as far as she was concerned. One that she'd want to keep for herself, apart from anything else that happened in her relationship with Marcus. He was propped up against the doorway, one leg bent at an angle against the door, having loosened his tie, his discarded jacket slung over his shoulder. Marcus caught her attention as she spoke to the photographer.

Flowers still in hand, she turned from Sean and took a step closer to Marcus to hear what he had to say. His free hand took hers and she went to him. Sean was calling out for them to hold it while he scrambled to get the shot. When Marc's arm went to her waist, she automatically put her hand on his chest and stretched up to kiss him. Coming to life, Marc let his jacket fall to the floor and pulled her into an embrace, waving Sean Cullen away.

It was a gentle kiss, full of the promise of more to come, and the softness in his blue eyes nearly melted her on the spot.

CHAPTER TWENTY-FOUR

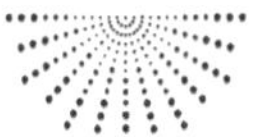

*A*ll through the reception, Laura's mind kept racing ahead in anticipation, until she and Marcus could be alone. She ate, but later wouldn't remember any of what was on the menu. Every time Marc looked her way, she couldn't break his gaze. More than once, the heat in his eyes meant she had to fan herself with the dinner menu. Brushing against her often, he showered her with delicious little kisses that sent bursts of electrical shock waves spiralling throughout her body.

Speeches were made and the cake was cut. Thankfully, there was no dancing. Danielle offered to escort her to the bathroom to help with the dress, but she declined the offer, sure she could manage on her own. It was a relief to be able to get a little bit of time to gather her thoughts.

Rounding the corner on her return, she saw Marcus in conversation with his father outside the function room. David Bradley clapped his son on the shoulder. Nodding, he acknowledged Laura and walked away.

Reaching Marcus, she knew instinctively something was wrong. She searched his face for a clue as he took her arms.

"It's Sir Charles, Laura. Dad just got word from London that he's had a massive stroke and is not expected to live."

"Oh Marc, no."

Marcus shook his head unable to comprehend the news himself.

"What happened?"

"Apparently it was a routine operation and he was making a good recovery, then he developed a blood clot..."

She put her arms around him and held him, remembering Marc telling her how his parents had met Charles Ogilvie while studying medicine together at the University of Queensland. Charles had been on an exchange program and had become friends with both David and Emma, so much so that he had flown back to Brisbane to be best man at their wedding soon after graduation.

Marc's parents had then moved to the UK for five years and worked at the same hospital as Charles. Emma had been pregnant with Stephen when they returned, and their firstborn was given "Charles" as his middle name. Charles had gone on to marry Helen and have three children of his own. The overwhelming need he had seen in some of the countries he had visited led him to start Medi-Aid over two decades ago. He had been knighted by the Queen for his tireless work to establish Medi-Aid in over fifteen countries.

"Are you going over?"

"Dad is trying to see if he can arrange flights for the four of us now."

"Four of us?'

"Dad and Stephen, you and I."

He saw the colour drain from her face. She swallowed hard. "Oh Marc, I can't."

"Of course you have to come. There's no way I'm leaving my new bride behind."

Laura took a breath. "I don't think you will have much choice."

"Why ever not?"

"Because I didn't get my passport renewed."

"You what?"

"I'm sorry, Marc, I clean forgot about getting it fixed. There's not six months' validity left."

He swore softly. "I'm not going without you. I'll wait until we can get it sorted on Monday. We can arrange an emergency passport."

"Marc it's okay. Go, please. You need to be in London. It may be too late if you wait for me to be able to go with you."

"I don't know what to say."

"It's okay, I understand, but please go."

"But…"

"But nothing. I can wait. I'll be fine. Really."

THE RECEPTION WAS ALREADY WRAPPING up. Marcus didn't want to have to explain the situation to all of the guests. Unaware of the truth, they farewelled the newlyweds.

As soon as he was able, Stephen returned after taking Danielle and the family to their hotel rooms. Packed and ready to go, he joined his father and brother in a private lounge area. Laura sat holding Marc's hand as his father talked on the telephone.

"Looks like we are in business," David commented as he hung up. The two men slipped out to allow Laura and Marcus a few minutes alone.

Words were inadequate as they just held each other for a long time. His farewell kiss was achingly tender. She let him go, reluctantly, but knowing it was what she had to do. She sat where she was for a long time after they left for the airport.

THE HONEYMOON SUITE was eerily quiet. A huge arrangement of flowers dwarfed the small table across from the bed. The note was handwritten on hotel stationery. Who knows when he had managed to arrange them?

Sorry to make you wait. I hope I won't need to be away for long. Marc

Surprisingly, she slept well, spending the next morning with Danielle and the children before they flew home.

Her new sister-in-law hugged her. "Are you sure you are going to be alright?"

"There will be a media storm for sure when they find out the groom did a runner on his wedding night. You had best lay low with the kids for a while, and don't feel obliged to make any comment."

"What about you?"

"I'm getting well-versed in handling the media. You guys had best be out of here before it hits the fan."

"You take care, okay."

"Sure."

Laura decided to pre-empt things by releasing a statement before she flew north, which was quickly picked up by media outlets around the country.

"Doctor Marcus Bradley has made a mercy dash to the United Kingdom with his father and brother to be with the family of Medi-Aid founder, Sir Charles Ogilvie, after he suffered a stroke late yesterday, Queensland time. Bradley received word during his wedding reception that mentor and family friend Charles Ogilvie had a massive stroke following routine surgery and was not expected to live. Due to unforeseen circumstances, his wife, Laura Bradley, has stayed behind in Australia. The Bradley family would ask the media and public to respect their privacy at this difficult time."

LAURA WAS wary when her plane touched down in Cairns.

Marc's colleague Susan Walsh and her husband Tim had arrived back from the wedding on an earlier plane. She was grateful they would be meeting her flight and putting her up for a few days; she would continue on to the apartment in a few days when the dust had settled.

Laura was relieved to see their faces in the waiting area. They each gave her a hug and kissed her on the cheek. Tim grabbed her bags from the carousel, and they headed out of the terminal. She was relieved not to have seen any cameras—not that she took time to scope out the area, just wanting to get out of the public space.

The couple had a neat lowset cul-de-sac home in a new gated community. Their high boundary walls provided an extra layer of privacy for Laura. Tim drove straight into the garage and the automatic door closed behind them. Their guest breathed a sigh of relief, pleased to be out of the public eye.

After settling into her room, Laura joined her hosts in their well-appointed kitchen and thanked them for their support.

Laura was absolutely horrified by the headlines in the tabloids the next day. There was a somewhat blurry photo of Tim giving her a kiss. Susan had been conveniently cropped out of the photo and the implication was that she'd taken up with a mystery man as soon as her new husband was out of the country.

"Oh Tim, I'm so sorry you got caught up in all of this."

He thought it was hilarious, although Laura couldn't see why.

"It doesn't take much to skew the truth, does it? Don't worry, it will all be forgotten in a couple of days, and they'll move on to another celebrity scandal of their own creation."

When Marcus finally made contact with her, he sounded unbelievably weary.

"How's Doctor Ogilvie?"

"His condition has deteriorated in the last couple of days. I don't think the end is far off now."

"I'm glad you got there in time."

"Yeah, me too, but the media has been giving us a hard time. There was a crush of them waiting to pounce as we left the hospital. I feel sorry for Helen and the family. They don't need all this crap at the moment. I think Dad and Stephen have copped a bit of flak as well."

Laura swallowed and made a confession. "Marc, there was a compromising photo in the papers here." She went on in a hurry, "They published a photo of Tim giving me a hello kiss at the airport and cut Susan out of the photo. They were trying to make out I had taken up with someone as soon as you left the country—"

Marc cut in, "Actually, it was in the tabloids here as well. That was the main focus of the paparazzi at the hospital. Tim already called and gave me a heads up, so I wasn't taken by surprise. Look, it wasn't ideal, I'll admit, but something like this was bound to happen. We've had a dream run as far as the publicity is concerned."

She was relieved he was taking it so calmly.

MARCUS CALLED his new wife every day, talking briefly. He gained strength just from hearing her voice. After much discussion it was decided that Laura wouldn't travel to the UK to be with him when her new passport arrived. He needed to devote his time and energy to supporting Helen and her family, as she and Charles had done for his father towards the end of his mother's battle with cancer.

It had been no secret at the time, but both mothers had been hopeful of a match between Marcus and the eldest Ogilvie daughter, Amanda. They were friends, sure, but there had never been that spark of attraction. Amanda had gone on to marry an investment banker and they had a young son. It was good to catch up with Amanda, her siblings and their partners. He just wished it wasn't in such difficult circumstances.

After the funeral, Marc stayed on a few more days with his father. Stephen had already flown back home to Townsville. There were going to be some inevitable issues with the Medi-Aid board following the unexpected death of the founder. They chaired a few meetings and met with various stakeholders. It looked like Marcus and his father may have their work cut out for them for the next few months, trying to sort everything out.

For the moment, though, he was pleased to finally be on the plane home. Well, back to Australia at least. He'd been summoned to Canberra to meet with government representatives about the funding for Medi-Aid in the southern hemisphere.

CHAPTER TWENTY-FIVE

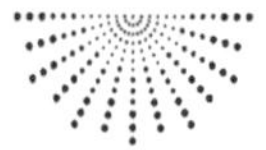

*L*aura noticed the box one day, after she'd returned to Marc's apartment. Why she hadn't seen it before she wasn't sure. She must have unpacked in a blur.

Pulling it from its place, she removed the lid to reveal its silken contents. She couldn't help but lift the material to her cheek, so smooth and cool. It seemed a shame for it to be sitting in the box, unused, from when she'd received it the afternoon of the wedding.

Making a decision, Laura took the nightgown and its matching wrap to the bathroom. After a shower, carefully washing and then drying her hair, she slipped into the beautiful material. The pencil-thin straps highlighted the sleek lines of her shoulders. The white bodice barely covered her breasts with its delicate lace and embroidery. The tiny fastenings at the front were barely visible. The length skimmed the floor. Pale blue edging at the waist matched the fine embroidery on the top. As Laura pulled the pale satin dressing gown up her long arms, she was amazed at Marc's uncanny ability to choose something so perfect in every way. The full-length mirror confirmed her thoughts. She felt very sensual, especially when she walked.

Not the sort of outfit you'd want to sit in front of the television with, but that is exactly what she did. The evening loomed before her, long and empty, so she filled it with the sights and sounds of late-night television. Stretching out on the charcoal sofa, obviously purchased to accommodate Marc's long frame, she made herself comfortable, settling in for a marathon session.

THE ROOM WAS in darkness when Laura woke. She had no idea of the time. As she stirred, she realised she was covered with a blanket and the television was silent. Gingerly, she got up, running fingers through sleep-tousled hair. There was a light on elsewhere. Marcus must be back.

She found him, sitting motionless at the dining table. His jacket had been slung carelessly over the chair back; his tie had fallen to the floor. His sleeves were rolled up, the top shirt buttons were undone. His elbows were on the table with his head in one hand. The other was still wrapped around a long-empty coffee mug.

She wondered how long he had been there, lost in thought. Weary.

She walked up and put a hand lightly on his shoulder. "Marc, are you okay?"

He seemed not to have heard. She noticed some movement. He raised his head, staring at the wall opposite before closing his eyes. Without quite realising what she was doing, Laura moved closer and began to massage the tight muscles along his shoulders.

Eventually he spoke. "I've been in marathon talks with the government about setting up an Asia/Pacific base for Medi-Aid, here in Australia. But as much as they sympathised with me, there was nothing they were prepared to do to help. They feel it would be too costly and time consuming, and that the money could be better spent at the coalface. Speaking of which, they have decided they won't match dollar-for-dollar everything we've managed to raise. They seem to think we're doing well enough without government help."

Laura leaned over and kissed him on the cheek, to offer some sympathy. But she was unable to stop her hand as it slid down the front of his shirt. He stopped her with his own hand.

"Please don't do that unless you are prepared to follow through. I've had about enough rejection for one day."

Laura's response was to continue with gentle insistence what she had been doing.

Getting up from the table, Marcus turned to her, his eyes seeking hers. "Are you sure you want this?"

Laura could feel her heart hammering wildly in her chest. How could she find enough words to tell him just how much she wanted this? Every part of her body, her very being, had been longing for this time. She hadn't been sure when or where, but she had known it would happen, and she was sure. Knowing that she would take whatever he gave her. Something to look back on when this was all over. She was prepared to offer him the key to her emotions. They had been held in check for far too long. It was time to let go and experience fully the depth of feeling she knew he aroused in her. It would be like jumping out of a boat into a churning sea. A sea of emotion she was prepared to let take her wherever it wanted.

As she nodded, she watched the weariness lift from him. He took her hand and led her wordlessly to the bedroom. The bedside lamps glowed softly as she had left them earlier. The huge bed had its covers turned down, waiting. But she wouldn't be alone tonight.

Marcus slid her wrap down easily. She waited as his eyes roved over her silken figure. He obviously approved. Reaching out, he cupped her face with his hand and stroked her cheek and felt the softness of her hair. As he kissed her forehead, his finger lightly trailed down her neck and across her shoulder causing an involuntary shiver. Hooking the strap, he tugged it down her shoulder.

His voice was husky, thick with emotion. "Sometimes, I wondered if we would ever get to this moment … it's been a long wait…"

Marcus took possession of her waiting lips, slowly and deliberately. She responded, enjoying every sensation he aroused. Savouring the taste of coffee and mint on his breath. He moved across her face, raining kisses as he went. He didn't need to fan the flame of desire; it was already threatening to consume her. The trail of fire he left across her shoulder caused her to moan as he tangled his hand in her hair and pulled her closer.

The fastenings on the gown gave way easily to his expert fingers and his eyes followed the sheath of material as it slipped to the carpet. He took in every part of her figure. He was hungry for her, starving, wanting to devour her quickly, but he held off, needing to enjoy every part of her.

"You are so beautiful," he whispered before closing the gap between them. His hands caressed and tantalised her as they swept over her body.

Her own fumbled with his shirt buttons before pushing it down over his broad shoulders. She kissed his neck, his shoulders, his chest, before he claimed her lips again. Her hands reached for his neck to pull him closer. The touch of skin against skin sent shock waves of desire coursing through her from top to bottom and back again. With growing urgency, Marc released his belt as he situated her onto the bed, where he quickly joined her.

IT WAS the smell of fresh coffee brewing that eventually enticed Laura awake. The bed beside her was empty. She reached for Marc's thick navy bathrobe and snuggled into it, tying it loosely before padding out to the kitchen.

Wearing just a pair of dark blue satin boxer shorts, Marc was cutting up fruit for a breakfast platter. Pausing in the doorway, she watched her husband in delight at the way he moved. He was so good-looking, he took her breath away. Stealing up behind him she ran her hands wickedly over his back, around and up and down his chest, chuckling at his involuntary response.

"You little minx," he teased, holding his arm up as she slipped around next to him. "I'll end up slicing my fingers if you don't stop."

She didn't stop. He tossed the knife onto the cutting board.

"I think," he said, as he caught her around the waist and swung her up onto the bench near where he was working, "you had better sit up here where I can keep an eye on you." He attempted to go on with the job at hand, but she could tell she was having an unsettling effect on him.

Smiling seductively, she leaned across and swiped a strawberry and popped it in her mouth, the edge of the robe gaping open.

"You're not wearing anything under that, are you?"

She shook her head slowly, her face lighting up as he groaned and abandoned the task. Undoing the tie on the robe he slipped his hands inside around her body and pulled her off the bench and onto the floor, kissing her all the while. Once the robe had been dispensed with, he lowered her onto its folds and covered her body with his own. The cold hardness of the floor at her back contrasted with the heat and passion of the man on top of her. She arched her body towards him, urging him to fulfil her need for him, which he did as she groaned his name in pleasure.

LATER, much later, they enjoyed breakfast out on the balcony. Laura had changed into a white camisole and shorts set that made her legs seem to go on forever. The matching wrap slipped off one shoulder as she leaned back with a bowl of fruit resting on her chest.

He couldn't help himself and pushed his chair closer to hers so he could lean over and nuzzle her cheek, and treat her to a smorgasbord of kisses. "I think," he said as he stroked her hair, kissing her softly, "that even though I'm back in the country... I'll make sure there's nothing scheduled for the rest of the week. Suddenly... I find work... very.... unappealing."

Marcus rose to go inside; he knew Laura was hot on his heels. He tried to make the phone call, with Laura doing her best to distract him. She didn't have to try too hard. Marcus attempted to fend off her advances as he spoke to his receptionist. Turning his back, he leaned on the arm of the sofa, phone in one hand, receiver in the other. She ducked underneath his arm and wrapped her own around his neck and teasingly started to plant kisses quietly on his cheek, then his neck and shoulders, slowly, tantalisingly, moving purposefully down his frame.

She was killing him.

Pausing to gauge his reaction, Laura was rewarded by seeing him rapidly losing his composure. He barely managed to finish the call. She wasn't quite fast enough to escape his clutches as he hung up. Pushing her arms behind her back, he pulled her hard up against him.

"I'm going to have to punish you for that," he growled, his eyes glinting with mischief as he sent her backwards onto the sofa, pinning her between the back of the sofa and his body. She squirmed and wriggled as he enjoyed watching her wait to see what he would do next. Her tongue darted out to lick her lips. He groaned and bent his head as if to kiss her waiting lips, then started to tickle her unmercifully until she implored him to stop.

"Not until you apologise." He grinned at her.

"Okay, okay you win, I'm sorry."

He stopped his torment. "That's better." His hands moved instead to caress her and invite a response as his lips sought hers, arousing every part of him. She stopped wriggling and started to move to the rhythm of his body.

~

Waking up to find Marcus lying next to her was a feeling Laura couldn't describe. To be enfolded in his arms and listen to his heartbeat and know that he was her husband, even if for a limited time, was very gratifying. She was totally relaxed and extremely happy.

"How did you sleep?" Marc murmured into her hair, holding her close.

"Mmmm… very well," she told him, shifting slightly into a more comfortable position.

"No nightmares?"

She shook her head. "I haven't had any for a while now."

"Looks like you could be on your way to a full recovery."

"Thanks to you, Doctor Bradley." She tipped her head back to kiss him on the chin and snuggled into his arms.

"You know, I think I'm almost grateful we were kidnapped," he confessed. "It did bring us together."

Laura wasn't so convinced.

He went on. "You know I really didn't need to take you on that trip. Kay wasn't that sick. I was just trying to engineer a way of spending some time with you. When she said she wasn't feeling a hundred per cent, I saw an opportunity."

"So, you could have been lying here with her instead of me?"

"Hardly." He chuckled. "The outcome would have been very different, believe me… but when I saw you that first day, I was surprised to find myself so attracted to you. Then I was so frustrated when you performed so badly in theatre, I wondered if they'd taken one look at you and forgotten to check your references."

"You did check out my credentials?"

"Of course, and naturally I was impressed. But when I tried to make amends you didn't want anything to do with me… you really hated me, didn't you?"

Laura laughed and owned up. "On the contrary, Marc. I

think the moment I looked up and saw you at the counter I was gone. In a couple of minutes, you managed to create havoc with every part of me. It was so fast and so bad; I couldn't concentrate in theatre and that worried me. I was denying anything could possibly happen that quickly, so I tried to keep out of your way to lessen the emotional turmoil… but… it didn't work very well. When you cornered me in the staffroom that night, I realised what was happening."

Marc let her go and rolled up onto his elbow so he could look at her better, obviously taken aback by her admission. "You little fool," he teased, "to think you felt the same way all along…" He sighed. "So much wasted time."

"I probably would have run a mile though."

He shook his head in mock despair.

"Was it worth the wait?" Laura asked him quietly. Leaning down, his kiss told her all she needed to know. That day they didn't leave the bedroom.

Laura decided if a movie ever eventuated about their ordeal —and there were already several groups clamouring for the film rights—the next few days would be depicted as a montage of overlapping images, accompanied by some appropriately orchestrated music. That was how she wanted to remember those precious moments, like a scene from a favourite movie she could replay over and over whenever she had a mind to.

Even when Marcus went back to work to catch up on his patient caseload, they were still able to snatch some golden moments together.

MARC WAS LOOKING FORWARD to getting home to Laura. His wife. Drained from theatre, he had to work harder to concentrate on what he should be doing, not on what he'd rather be doing.

Every so often, something Laura had said or done would

come to mind and he would have to push it aside and refocus on the task at hand. By the time he drove back to the apartment, he was more tired than usual. The elevator seemed to take forever. He couldn't get in the door fast enough.

She was sitting in the lounge. Reading. Waiting. Wearing a long, flowing, multi-print caftan. Her hair loose around her shoulders. Laura looked up at him, smiling, as he walked over to her. He pulled her gently into his arms and kissed her. He was hungry not only for dinner, but for her.

"How was your day?" she said.

No point hiding the truth. "Tough day at the office. Kept thinking about my gorgeous wife, so I had to work doubly hard to stay in the zone."

"Hmm… sorry about that."

"Don't be." He just wanted to hold her. Breathe in the scent of her.

After a few minutes, she eased herself out of his arms. "Go have a shower, I'll serve dinner."

"You could always join me."

"Tempting, but no."

He snatched another kiss before going through to the bathroom.

LATER AS SHE curled up next to him on the sofa, Marc made a suggestion. "How would you like to do some theatre work?"

"What, with you?"

"No, I'm afraid you'd be too distracting, but Roger Lambert could use another pair of hands at the moment. He'd be happy to give you a trial."

"Are you sure that would be a good idea?"

"You might as well keep your hand in. Who knows how long it will be before you get back to your job in Brisbane?"

And there it was. A reference to the future, and one that

obviously wasn't in Cairns with him. Laura knew the marriage wasn't supposed to go the distance. But still, she'd thought over the last couple of weeks that things had shifted between them. She'd assumed—no, she'd hoped—that maybe, just maybe, this marriage would not be a short-term thing. She had even started thinking long-term, like starting a family.

Looked like it was just her that felt that way. She had to decide what, if anything, she was going to do about it. Enjoy him while she had him? Every single moment? Even though the prospect of them not being married was becoming so much harder to accept. What else could she do?

LAURA MET with Doctor Lambert and his team, and was soon into the thick of things. She didn't take long to adapt to his preferred modus operandi and enjoyed working again, even if it was for a few—albeit very long—days. Marc arranged for Mrs Knight to come in and prepare meals, so there was one less thing to worry about after a tiring day.

"Your wife," Roger Lambert told his colleague, "is one of the best I have worked with. Are you sure I can't have her with me on a permanent basis?"

"Sorry mate, not in the short term. Maybe down the track when this Medi-Aid circus dies down."

CHAPTER TWENTY-SIX

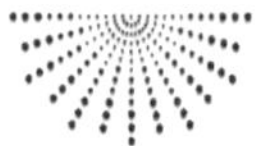

Marcus thought he could hear Laura talking to someone. He ventured down the hallway. She was on the phone, and what he heard stopped him in his tracks.

"Peter, darling, you know it will be okay. It's only for a little while longer and then it will be all over... Just hang in there... You can do this... You know how much you mean to me... Then it will be a whole new life."

He swallowed hard, not believing what he was hearing. Laura had never mentioned a Peter before. And it seemed that she couldn't wait for their marriage to be over so she could go back to him. Here he was, thinking she was in love with him, and all the while she was wishing she was with another man.

Marc retreated to his study and sat down heavily, his mind chaotic. They were good together, he knew. The thought of Laura being with another man and not him filled him with a gut-wrenching pain. It couldn't be true, surely?

He loved her. But he needed to think. To get away and get some perspective. It wasn't long before he had the answer he needed.

~

LAURA HAD BEEN SPENDING time with Doctor Susan Walsh, forging a firm friendship. Tonight, she and Marc were having dinner with Susan and Tim at their home. She was concerned about Marc. The last few days he had become distant. Maybe his heavy surgery schedule was starting to catch up with him. Then, there were all the requests still pouring in for them to appear, here, there and everywhere around the country. The media were still captivated by them. Especially since the wedding photos had been published.

Maybe he was tiring of the whole thing. Maybe he was tiring of their fake marriage and was looking for a way out—impossible with the demand for public appearances still so high. She'd made up her mind to talk with him once they went home tonight.

Midway through dinner that night, however, Marc dropped a bombshell.

"The Medi-Aid board has been in disarray since Sir Charles died. There's been some factional infighting…"

"Any financial troubles?" Tim wanted to know.

"No, thankfully, but they have asked me to take on the role of president in an acting capacity in the short term, to help mediate between the sides and help transition into the future, whatever that might look like. It's all uncertain at the moment."

"How long could that take?"

"I have no idea. Depends on how much the various stakeholders are prepared to compromise and accommodate each other's views. I expect I'll have to canvass the views from all of the locations."

Laura quietly put her fork down. "When do you leave?" she asked, barely able to get the words out.

He didn't look up when he replied. "I have to fly out first thing in the morning."

Susan and Tim exchanged glances as they realised from Laura's apparent shock that the subject hadn't been discussed.

Laura tried to keep her voice on an even keel. Wary about losing it in front of their friends. "So, when were you planning to tell me?"

"I just did. The travel arrangements were only confirmed before we left to come here." He continued to eat, ignoring the silence at the table.

~

"I'LL CALL you in a day or so," Susan told her on the side as Laura and Marc prepared to leave.

Laura nodded dumbly before accepting a quick hug. The trip back to the apartment was strained. Marcus opened the door, standing aside to let her enter first. He followed her along the hallway.

"I've got a lot of paperwork to finish. Don't wait up for me." Flipping the light on in the study, he shut the door behind him.

~

LAURA HEARD Marc's flight number being called over the PA system, and waited while he shoved his papers back into his briefcase and slung his jacket over his shoulder before picking up his cabin bag.

Her itinerary was set out for weeks ahead. Marcus had spent some time going over it with her, leaving notes for how to answer questions about his absence overseas. He had been brusque and businesslike, and Laura found it hard to believe it was the same man she had shared a bed with—and the love-making that had gone along with it.

He hadn't shared it with her last night. The other side of the bed hadn't been slept in.

Confused and hurt, Laura retreated into herself, afraid to say anything. Afraid of the response. Had she imagined the depth of his feelings for her? Had he tired of their physical relationship already? She had thought he wanted her as much as she wanted him.

Wanted, or loved? Laura realised that her feelings went further than just wanting him. She was deeply in love with Marcus, but in the whole time they had been together she had never heard him give any indication he returned those deeper feelings. Laura chided herself for expecting more of him. She had been prepared to accept whatever he offered her. But now she conceded it wasn't enough. It would never satisfy her. She was longing to be part of his life on a permanent basis, the mother of his children. The publicity machine would soon wind down, and with it they would go their separate ways. All that would be left: her memories to treasure and some magazine articles.

Marcus dropped a light kiss on her head and left her in the passenger lounge. Wrapped her arms around herself, she waited until the plane taxied along the runway. As it lifted off the tarmac, Laura turned to go, pulling the BMW key out of her purse. At least he trusted her enough to drive his car and she wanted to enjoy every minute.

Wanting to and being able to, as it turned out, were two different things. She had hardly got out of town when she had to pull over to the side of the road, in tears. Marcus had travelled before, but this time it was different. They had shared so much in the last few weeks, and now she didn't know where she stood.

TWO DAYS LATER, Laura was on a plane herself. This time the going was a lot tougher. The schedule was gruelling. It kept her tired and on the go. From town to town she went. Big venues, little halls, large crowds, small gatherings of just a handful of locals. Laura hardly had time to catch her breath. Week after week it went on. The fatigue started to set in. The nightmares returned.

She hadn't heard from Marcus, personally. She never told Danielle or Susan the truth when they spoke on the phone. Any news was gleaned from them, or via reporters and newspaper stories.

MARCUS WORKED HARD. The disarray from the untimely death of Charles Ogilvie pushed him where he didn't want to be. Acting president was an all-consuming role, as he tried to accommodate the varying needs of the different countries. He travelled more than he cared to, more than he wanted to.

Laura's sad face when he left her at the airport haunted him. He should call her. See how she was going. But he couldn't bring himself to deal with his feelings; he just shoved them way down. There was enough on his plate.

Nights were the worst. He always thought of her, the time they'd spent together. He wanted to call, but he just couldn't bring himself to do it. Maybe he was scared that she would tell him she was leaving him for Peter. He'd thought they were amazing together. He should "man up" and just deal with it. The longer he was away from Australia, the easier it became to ignore.

SHE SHOULDN'T HAVE BEEN surprised when she came down with a stomach virus. There were so many bugs around, it was only a matter of time before she succumbed. Being so tired, she was hit with a double whammy.

For a couple of days, she soldiered on, but it was too much. Stuck in bed in a motel somewhere in a strange city wasn't any fun. Once the diarrhea settled, then the vomiting started. She was grateful she didn't get both at once.

After a couple of days, Laura was so weak she could hardly drag herself around. Despite cutting back on her speaking engagements and other public appearances, Laura couldn't shake her illness.

In the end, she cancelled the lot and flew back to Cairns. She unpacked in the spare bedroom of the apartment, unable to face using the main bedroom without Marcus to share it with. A week of R&R helped her to recover no end, but she was still not a hundred percent.

Not knowing who else she could trust, and needing a friendly face to talk to, Laura made a medical appointment to see her friend, Susan Walsh.

Sitting across from Susan, Laura told her what she had been through the last little while and asked for some advice. Susan listened to her carefully.

"Laura, have you ever thought you might be pregnant?" she suggested gently.

"I… er, no… it never crossed my mind." Laura gaped.

"Well let's just do some tests before we jump to any conclusions."

A short time later, Laura looked in disbelief at the positive result.

"Congratulations Laura, you are going to be a mum."

Laura slumped back in her seat. "How could that have happened? It's not like we didn't…"

"Laura, you know that no contraception is one hundred per cent reliable, right?"

"I know that… but I mean… I never expected… this is all too soon… Marc never… we never thought of starting a family… oh, my…"

Susan came around the desk and put a comforting arm around her shoulder. "You're not the first couple it's happened to, and you certainly won't be the last. Everything will work out, you'll see, once you get past the initial shock. I'm sure Marc will be over the moon. When will you tell him?"

Laura felt all the colour drain from her face. Of course she'd have to tell him, but what would he think, what would he say? Things were complicated enough as they were without this added. She realised Susan had asked a question.

"Are you sure you had no idea?"

"None. My system's been out of whack since the kidnapping. There was no way of knowing when things would settle down. I've been so busy. Any feelings of being unwell I just put down to the bug I had and the long hours I've been putting in."

"Okay, I think I'd better do a quick scan so we can get some idea of dates." Susan went to get a trolley and pushed it over to the examination table. Reaching up, she tugged the curtains loose and pulled them along the track. Laura stripped off as she was told, and waited for the doctor to return. Flicking on the small screen, Susan took a plastic bottle and squeezed some gel onto the transducer, then rubbed it across Laura's abdomen. Susan studied the grey movement on the screen. "Ah there we are. It would be better, though, if you had a full bladder." She swivelled the monitor for Laura to see. "This is your baby, Laura. It probably doesn't seem more than a grainy blur, but there's the head, see, and the spine. Now if I can just get a measurement here—okay, done." She scribbled on a notepad. "Right-o, let's go for some more measurements."

Laura watched in amazement. A baby. Hers and Marc's child. She was overwhelmed.

Susan checked her figures. "According to these calculations you are about ten weeks along."

Laura nodded dumbly.

"I want to make arrangements for you to go and have another scan at eighteen weeks. We can get it done here in the centre if you like. Doctor Neville has state-of-the-art equipment. Makes my machine look like a child's toy—though it gets the job done."

Susan crossed to her desk and began writing while Laura dressed. "I think you had better slow down for a while until you feel better."

"No, I'd rather keep busy. It's not like there's anything seriously wrong. I'm having a baby—it's a natural thing. Pregnant women can keep working right up until the birth. It shouldn't be a problem at all. Now that I know, I can just get on with it. I shouldn't have to reorganise my schedule too much."

"Laura, you're talking to an obstetrician, I know all that. But not many women have been through a three-week kidnapping ordeal, and the publicity mill you've been on since then has been constant, and you managed to get married in the middle of all that. My opinion as a doctor and friend is that you need to relax and take it easy, put your feet up for a while so you can enjoy being a wife and an expectant mother and not public property. What's your schedule for the next few weeks?"

Laura told her without batting an eye.

"Good grief, I can't believe Marcus could have set such a demanding itinerary."

Laura shrugged. "We have to milk the publicity for Medi-Aid while we can. Who knows how much longer it will last?"

"Laura, your health is more important than publicity for Medi-Aid. I've a good mind to call Marcus and give him a piece of my mind."

"No." Laura was adamant. "It's okay, Susan, it's what I agreed to do. I can't back out now."

"I'm sure he'll understand, given the circumstances."

"He might think I've done it on purpose to get out of our arrangement," Laura replied quietly, without thinking.

"Whoa there, what are you talking about, Laura? What arrangement?"

Laura knew she had said too much. She dropped her head and fiddled with the hem of her shirt.

After a couple of minutes' silence, Susan spoke. "Laura are you going to tell me what's going on here?"

Laura shrugged helplessly, not knowing what she should do. She looked up at Susan, and tears began to prick at her eyes.

Susan picked up the phone and cancelled her other appointments, obviously concerned at the torment in her friend's eyes. Then she got down next to Laura and gently prodded her for more information.

Laura was hesitant at first and then it all came out in a torrent, the words falling out all over the place.

Susan listened with eyes of disbelief at what she was hearing. "So, let me get this straight." She stood up and leaned back on her desk. "You're telling me that everything that's happened has been part of a publicity campaign to raise money for Medi-Aid?" Laura nodded. "The engagement and the wedding?"

Laura nodded again. "It will end in divorce somewhere down the track."

"You're kidding?"

"No, that was part of the deal."

"Laura that sounds so unlike the Marcus I know, I don't know what to say. Maybe the amount of money involved clouded his judgement, but that doesn't negate his behaviour towards you. It was plain wrong. But I want to know how you feel about 'the deal'?"

"Well… I… um… agreed to go along with it to a certain point, but once the publicity machine got going, everything snowballed. I just kept getting in deeper and deeper and, well, I just didn't put a stop to it."

"Why not?"

"I tried, but in the end, I realised I didn't really want to… because I started caring for Marc…"

"Do you love him, Laura?"

She nodded. "I just wanted to be with him… the circumstances didn't matter anymore… I decided to accept however long we had together and enjoy every moment."

"Looks like you've been doing that."

Laura smiled ruefully. "To say this has complicated things a little is an understatement… I have no idea where this is headed now. But I do know that this baby will be a living reminder to me of the relationship we had, even if only for a short while."

"Will you be satisfied with that?"

"I may well have to be."

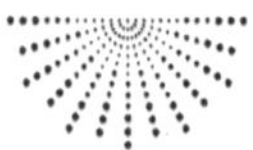

CHAPTER TWENTY-SEVEN

*A*s she waited in the wings, it was a relief to Laura that it was her last speaking engagement for some time. Televised. She was going to tell the gathered audience it was because of some suitably vague doctor's orders, which in a way it was. But the truth was, she would not be able to hide her pregnancy much longer, and she didn't want to have to deal with the fallout if the general public found out.

Marc still didn't know, but she hadn't gone out of her way to try and track him down. Too scared of what his reaction might be.

MARCUS SAT on the end of yet another hotel bed, flicking from channel to channel on the small room's television set. He could finally see some light at the end of the Medi-Aid tunnel. There was a plane ticket for home on the bedside table. Home to what, exactly, he wasn't sure.

The last few months had taken a huge toll on him—physically and emotionally. Laura. He missed her so much. Normally in life he was confident and self-assured. But this? Every preconceived thought went out the window. He said and did things he should not have. He had no idea how she would receive him if he saw her again and he needed to, badly—to try and sort something out.

Yes, he had promised her a divorce as part of the deal—if that's what she wanted. Marcus needed to hear it for himself from her own lips. There was no way he wanted that, even though he was haunted by the fact she may have taken a lover. The whole time they had been together there had never been a hint of someone else.

It was confusing, but he had heard what he had heard. Laura's words on the phone that day chased themselves around in his brain every other night. Marc couldn't help but wonder if she was with Peter. No one he spoke to from back home ever mentioned anything untoward, but maybe they were just being kind.

Unable to settle, he lingered on a late-night news broadcast. Suddenly, his attention was caught by vision of Laura addressing a conference. The voice-over explained that she would be taking some time off on doctor's orders. As he watched his wife, he realised there was something different about her that he couldn't quite put his finger on. Marcus took a couple of steps closer to the screen, but the segment was gone.

It wasn't until later that night that the possibility dawned on him.

As soon as he was off the plane in Cairns, Marcus called Susan's direct number. He didn't mince his words, barely saying hello. "I need to talk to you about Laura. Have you been seeing her as a patient?"

"Sorry Marc, patient confidentiality, you know I'm not at liberty to pass information on."

He took that as a yes.

"Damn it, Susan, don't pull that on me, it's my wife you're talking about. I'm coming to see you in person. I'll be there in forty minutes."

He walked in the side entrance, to avoid the general public, and was pacing the empty consultation room when Susan arrived. She indicated the chair across from her desk as she sat down, but he ignored her.

"Do you know where Laura is? She seems to have disappeared."

"Sorry, no."

"There was a news report recently that said she had to rest on doctor's orders. Would you be that doctor by any chance?"

"Laura is exhausted, Marc. That schedule you had her on was totally ridiculous. She got sick a couple of months back and hasn't been able to fully recover. She needs to slow down and take it easy for a while so she can recover her health."

He leaned back against the examination bench with his arms folded across his chest, regarding Susan. Then he just threw it out there.

"Laura's pregnant, isn't she?" He watched Susan's reaction, but she gave nothing away.

"Marc, I can't discuss a patient with you without their consent." He crossed to her desk and leaned both hands on the edge.

"Susan, please, I need to know," he begged.

She nodded at him and he sat down heavily, slightly stunned.

"How far?"

"You could work that out for yourself. Just before you left to go overseas."

"Assuming the baby is mine."

Susan was shocked at his comment. "Where on earth did you get that thought from?"

"I overheard her talking on the phone to some bloke named Peter. Sounded like they were having an affair."

"Did you confront her about it?"

"No."

"Well, you should have. That's a totally ludicrous assumption to make. I think you have jumped to a very wrong conclusion. Laura has never, ever mentioned even a hint of anyone else possibly being the father except for you… she loves you, Marc."

"She does?"

"Very much. She was worried how you would react when you found out." As he sat in stunned silence, she continued, "Laura told me the whole story."

"I see."

"I'm not going to pretend to understand why you did what you did, but you have to put a stop to it for both your sakes. You do love her, Marc, don't you?"

"Hell, yes."

"Well you had better find her and sort this out." Susan stood up and came around to where he was sitting. She put a hand on his shoulder.

"Thanks Susan. I will if I can find out where she's disappeared to."

MARC GOT the first available flight out of Cairns. He was still reeling. Susan had let him have it with both barrels and deservedly so. She had held nothing back and called him a couple of choice names into the bargain. Of course she was totally right. He had behaved abominably towards Laura. His wife. He needed to make amends, and he hoped it wasn't too late.

LAURA LET herself into the room at the resort. The same place she and Marcus had stayed after their return to Australia. Yes, she had to admit, she had charmed her way into getting a good deal. The resort manager was happy to accommodate her wishes for a quiet getaway from the public spotlight.

Laura was keen to lie low for a while. Leaning back on the closed door, she unconsciously rubbed her stomach, then headed for the bedroom to change into a cooler outfit.

As she surveyed her reflection a short time later, she realised she had really popped out in the last couple of weeks. The loose long-line chambray sleeveless button-through shirt and matching shorts were her first major concession to her changing figure—the first of many, she thought wryly.

She was feeling much better. Although bouts of nausea hit her unexpectedly from time to time, she wasn't overly troubled with health concerns. As she walked out to the dining room, she stopped short.

Marcus.

He was sitting on a lounge chair near the large sliding door that opened onto a private courtyard, which ultimately led down to the beach. Black trousers and his signature light blue button-down shirt, rolled up to mid-arm. His hair was a little longer. He looked good—tired but good—despite the dark circles under his eyes.

Laura.

Finally.

She looked good. Better than good actually. The loose shirt she wore hid her figure well, but there was no hiding the pregnancy glow.

Her initial shock at seeing him had been replaced with a wariness—not that he blamed her—he hadn't been in contact for weeks. Cut her off cold.

But as he looked at her standing there, he remembered how she fit against him, how she felt in his arms, how she tasted. He missed being with her in every sense of the word. He needed to get closer. To inhale the scent of her. But he forced himself to stay where he was. There was an underlying sadness in her, and he felt guilty, knowing he was the cause.

"Marcus, how did you…?" she trailed off.

"Your father told me you were here. I just told them at the front desk I'd come to surprise you, and they were happy to have someone let me in."

LAURA FELT a sudden wave of nausea and reached out to grab hold of the chair in front of her to steady herself.

Marcus was on his feet. "Are you alright?" Concern edged his voice.

"Yes," she lied. "Guess I didn't eat enough lunch."

As he walked towards her, Laura couldn't help but catch her breath. She had missed him so much. Here he was in the flesh, looking at her like… like what, exactly?

It was all she could do to stop herself from going to him. Gripping the back of the chair harder, hoping it would hide her bump for now, she shook her head to try and remember the reason she came to the coast.

"Why have you been hiding?"

"I couldn't go on with the lies and deception anymore, even if it was for a good cause. I can't do this anymore, Marcus. I want out."

"But I don't want you to go."

"Why not?" She licked her lips nervously, waiting for his response.

"I need you."

"You need me only for the PR campaign, to help raise money for Medi-Aid," she snapped as Marcus flinched. "How's this for a headline: 'Kidnap Couple split'? That should be good for a few more magazine stories. If you play it right, people will feel sorry for you and donate more to your cause."

"I've resigned from the Medi-Aid board."

She was surprised, and had to strain to hear what he said next.

"I didn't like being away so much… you see, Laura, I love you and want to be with you." By now he was standing a couple of centimetres away.

Laura couldn't believe what she was hearing. It was what she had longed for him to say.

"But," he went on, "I won't force you to stay if you don't feel the same way. I've behaved badly and I totally understand if you want a divorce." Silence hung heavy in the air.

She tried to weigh up everything in her mind. But in the end, her heart spoke for her.

"I'm afraid… I do love you, Marcus."

He waited to hear no more as he pulled her into his arms and kissed her hungrily. Laura returned his passion with hunger of her own.

SOMETIME LATER, as she stood revelling in the strength of his body against hers, she murmured.

"I don't understand why you left for overseas the way you did."

"I actually thought you might be having an affair."

She looked at him incredulously, shaking her head. "What? You're kidding! Where on earth did you get that idea from?"

"I overheard you talking to a Peter someone or other. How it would all be over soon and to hang in there and how life would never be the same…"

The light dawned on her. "Marc, you heard me talking to a Peter alright, but it's P.e.t.a, an old work colleague. Her husband is in the army and currently deployed overseas. She was pregnant with their first child and he wasn't going to be there for the birth. She was going through a rough patch, so I was trying to give her some encouragement over the phone."

"Really?"

"Yes. Really. They had a boy, by the way. Why didn't you just say something?"

"I couldn't bear to think it may have been true. I felt guilty for railroading you into the whole thing in the first place. I thought what we had might be just a physical attraction, and the phone call just played to my fears. The mess with Medi-Aid was a convenient way for me to give both of us some space, and try and figure out what to do."

"You never contacted me."

"At first I couldn't, and then the longer it went, the easier it was not to deal with it. I nearly didn't get on the plane in the first place. You looked so vulnerable and alone, I just wanted to say the hell with it, and take you in my arms and never let you go. But there was always that niggle at the back of my mind."

"Have you really cut ties with Medi-Aid?"

"For the moment. They want someone with a more 'hands on' approach, visiting teams in the field more often. With some of the trouble spots we're in currently, I'd be in constant danger. I think I'd be pushing my luck with each visit." He kissed her on the forehead. "I wouldn't like the added risk of our child growing up without a father."

"You know?" she asked looking up at him.

"Don't look so surprised, darling. I am a doctor after all, and as your husband I don't miss much about you. I saw you on a news report when you gave your last speech. When it said you were stopping due to doctor's orders, I put two and two together and went and confronted Susan as soon as I got back. She confirmed my suspicions, none too happily I might add. I was a little uptight. I was terrified when I found you had gone, that you might do something…"

Laura put a finger on his lips, shaking her head at him. "I

admit it was a huge shock. The possibility of being pregnant had never occurred to me. But in the end, I was happy to have a tangible reminder of how lucky I was to be with you, even if I couldn't have you—"

Marcus cut her off. "You have me." He bent to reclaim her lips. She watched as he gently placed a hand on her stomach, shaking his head at the wonder of it all.

"You don't mind becoming a father so soon?"

"Mind? You can't be serious. I'm thrilled!"

"I think I have another headline for you." She laughed as he looked at her. "How about 'Kidnap Couple's baby joy'?"

"Then we can retire from the glare of publicity, I hope."

"I'm not sure they will let us disappear completely, Marc."

"We'll see," he told her.

"They may want us to live happily ever after."

"Well, we can't disappoint the public, can we?"

She agreed as she reached up to kiss him again.

EPILOGUE

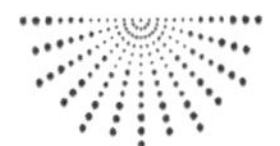

Marcus walked over with a long cool drink in each hand, and gave one to his wife as he joined her on the picnic rug at the bottom of their garden. Laura leaned across to give him a sweet, lingering kiss. Putting his glass aside he pulled her closer, intending to deepen the kiss, but Laura was distracted.

"Look, Marc!" she exclaimed.

He followed her gaze to where their daughter was pushing herself up into a standing position. Legs straight, backside in the air, her arms windmilled as she took a couple of wobbling steps then plopped back onto her padded behind. Grinning at her parents, she maneuvered onto her knees, crawling the distance to them over the grass with alarming speed. The little girl used her father's bent knee as support to haul herself to her feet again. Her mouth made a shocked "o" when she toppled over again.

Before she could squawk, Marc scooped her up and blew a raspberry on her bare tummy as her blue top rode up. Squealing with laughter, she wriggled as he held her close for a cuddle. Named after her two grandmothers, Emma Catherine had scored her mother's dark hair as well as her besotted father's blue eyes.

Wriggling, she held her chubby little baby hands out for her mother to take hold. Laura kissed the tiny fingers as the girl gurgled in pleasure.

A sigh of pure contentment escaped his lips as he delighted in his two girls. It had taken some doing, but they had finally found someone to take over the helm of Medi-Aid. Now Marcus could concentrate almost solely on his practice. While he had been a little reluctant to sell his apartment, they had settled well into their new family waterfront home in a quiet enclave closer to Cairns. The less time he spent commuting, the more time he could spend with Laura and Emma.

The media circus that had engulfed them after their return from Levati had thankfully run its course, but there would still be ongoing interest from time to time. Emma's first birthday in a couple of days was a case in point. There would be an obligatory photo call, but after that they would largely be left alone.

Their bestselling book had been optioned by a local production company in association with an American media conglomerate. They were waiting to read the script and to find out who had been cast to play their characters. They had chosen not to reveal all the details surrounding their story, but enough to keep everyone happy. Inevitably, there would be some more publicity down the track, but all in all they had fared well.

Laura leaned into him as he pulled Emma into his side and angled his head down to his wife.

"Have I told you lately how much I love you?" he murmured against her lips as he kissed her thoroughly.

The End

A NOTE FROM THE AUTHOR

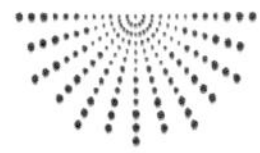

*D*ear Reader,

I hope you enjoyed the love story of Marcus and Laura—it has been rattling around in my head for a very long time.

If you can spare the time, I would greatly appreciate it if you could leave a review on your favourite platform. For an indie author like myself, it helps other readers to find my story.

To see photos of the places my stories are set, and connect with my writing journey and future stories, please sign up for my newsletter at

alisonjoywriter.com

Thanks for reading,
Alison

ABOUT THE AUTHOR

Alison Joy was born in Queensland, Australia, and her favourite colour is blue – except at State of Origin time.

A former early childhood teacher, she has always written books in her head. She finally plucked up the courage to embark on her own writing journey to publication and not worry so much about what other people might think. Her first book, *Brushstrokes of Love* set on the stunning coastline of southern Victoria, is available at all good online bookstores.

Alison is a musical theatre fan, a keen amateur photographer, and co-host of the Gracewriters Podcast for Christian writers. Discover more about Alison and sign up for her newsletter at:

alisonjoywriter.com

Follow her at:

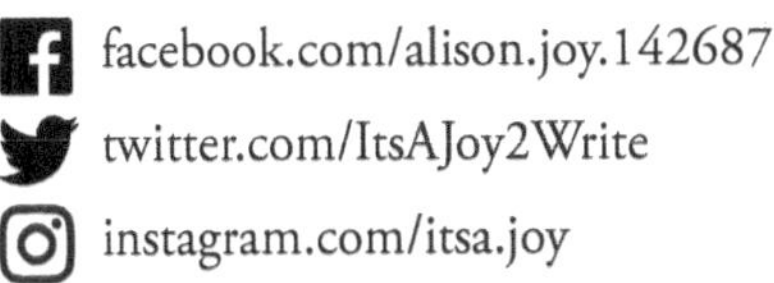

facebook.com/alison.joy.142687

twitter.com/ItsAJoy2Write

instagram.com/itsa.joy